'The king of the British hard-boiled thriller'
— *Times*

'Grips like a pair of regulation handcuffs'
— *Guardian*

'Reverberates like a gunshot'
— *Irish Times*

'Definitely one of the best'
— *Time Out*

'The mean streets of South London need their heroes tough.
Private eye Nick Sharman fits the bill'
— *Telegraph*

'Full of cars, girls, guns, strung out along the high sierras of Brixton
and Battersea, the Elephant and the North Peckham Estate, all
those jewels in the crown they call Sarf London'
— *Arena*

Other books by Mark Timlin

mark timlin

ashes by now

The Ninth Nick Sharman Thriller

NO EXIT PRESS

This edition published in 2015
by No Exit Press,
an imprint of Oldcastle Books
PO Box 394, Harpenden,
Herts, AL5 1XJ, UK

noexit.co.uk
@NoExitPress

A CIP catalogue record for this book is available from the British Library.

ISBN
978-1-84344-624-8 (print)
978-1-84344-625-5 (epub)
978-1-84344-626-2 (kindle)
978-1-84344-627-9 (pdf)

Typeset by Avocet Typeset, Somerton, Somerset
in 11pt Garamond
Printed in Great Britain by 4edge Limited, Essex

For more information about Crime Fiction go to crimetime.co.uk

Embrace your guilt.
For there your soul will grow
Jung

1

That morning, one not much different from any other, I let myself into my flat, kicked off my shoes and opened the fridge to find out what was left there in the way of alcohol.

I found a beer, opened it, sat on the sofa, lit a cigarette, and took a sip.

It was a little after nine and my head hurt.

I'd been out all night with a pair of strippers. Sorry, exotic dancers. Let's get the job description right. Sandi and Mandi they called themselves professionally. Both with *i's* on the end. Very exotic you must agree. Their real names were Tracey and Dawn. Which was Sandi and which was Mandi I never bothered to find out. Maybe it didn't matter. I'd met them a month or so previously in a drinking club in Peckham or Deptford. I can't remember which. That didn't matter either. All I *can* remember is that I'd woken up in bed with the pair of them the next day or the day after. Two hundred quid poorer, but a world of experience richer.

Don't get me wrong, Tracey and Dawn were all right as it goes. Better than any social workers I've ever met.

They were both about thirty I guess, although we didn't talk much about things like that. We didn't talk much about anything as a matter of fact.

They did a double act, at lunchtime round the few pubs in south-east London which could still get a licence for that sort of show, and in the last of the strip joints up west at night. It was a living I suppose. But then what did I ever know about earning a living?

If there were enough willing punters in the audience, or enough drunks, they'd pass around a pint pot, and when it was full of notes they'd get down and dirty on each other, and do another kind of double act. If the notes were of large enough denominations they'd let the geezers join in too. Most of them were too pissed to get it up by then, but everyone pretended they were having a right good time. It was something to tell the lads back at the office or on the dole queue.

Tracey and Dawn lived together in a ratty flat close to Wandsworth Common, and the night before they'd done the double act for me in the privacy of the drum. I just let them get on with it. It wasn't very long before they forgot I was there and really got going. I knew that was what they wanted anyway. I just left them to it, and went and ran cockroach races in the kitchen. I had quite an affinity for cockroaches in those days. I used to hate them, but I'd spent a diverting afternoon not so long ago with thousands of the little bastards, and since then I didn't mind them at all. In fact I often thought that the more I saw of people the fonder of cockroaches I became.

I'd dig a couple out from their nest in the central heating vent beside the kitchen stove and line them up for the two-metre dash. The loser got squashed and washed down the sink. Then I'd find another to race the winner, and so on. That way I figured I was breeding a faster strain of roach.

When I'd got tired of squashing insects I went back into the bedroom. Tracey and Dawn were naked on the bed. Their collection of vibrators, dildos, KY Jelly and other marital aids was scattered all around. Dawn was rolling a joint, and Tracey was cutting out a line of nose-bleed amphetamine sulphate on a plastic mirror.

'You been racing bugs again?' she asked.

I nodded.

'You're a weird bastard. I don't know why we put up with you. Want some of this? It's only cheap shit, but it's all I could get.'

I nodded again, sat on the bed next to her, accepted the cut down, red-and-white striped McDonald's straw she offered me, and took a hit of the speed.

It felt something like I imagine snorting ground glass would feel. Cheap shit was what it was, she'd been right about that. But it did the job.

'Got any dough, Nick?' said Dawn. 'We can't live on fucking air you know.'

I pulled some notes out of the back pocket of my jeans and threw them on the bed next to her. I suppose there was about fifty nicker there. She stopped rolling the joint, picked up the cash, counted it, pulled a face, tossed the money on the bedside table and went back to the spliff.

The speed started to kick in and I lit a cigarette. I knew I'd be grinding my teeth soon so I took a stick of Wrigley's off the table where Dawn had chucked the money, unwrapped it, put it in my mouth and started chewing.

'We going out?' said Dawn. 'I'm starving.'

I shrugged, took the joint from between her fingers and inhaled a mouthful of smoke. She'd loaded it right up, and I immediately felt the dope start to counter the speed.

'Let's get tarted up, go and have a drink, and then some Chinese,' said Dawn.

Tracey thought about it, which took a while, but with Tracey thinking always did. 'That's a good idea,' she said eventually. 'You up for it, Nick?'

I nodded yet again.

'Right,' said Tracey, and jumped off the bed. 'That's what we'll do then.'

2

I stayed seated on the bed and watched them get ready to go out. Sometimes I think that watching women get dressed is hornier than watching them get undressed. It was with these two anyway. They were professional undressers. They were used to it. And when they did it in front of me, it was like I was just another punter. Which I was. But when they got dressed it was more intimate. I could imagine they weren't just there for the money, and the feeling seemed to get to them too. They appeared younger, more innocent and less hard. I expect it was just my imagination, but I didn't care.

Dawn put on a low-cut black bra which pushed her quite spectacular breasts up and apart, hitched a black suspender belt around her waist, rolled black fishnet stockings up her legs and fastened them tight. Over the bra she wore a thin white shirt, through which you could clearly see the outline of what was underneath. Then she struggled into a short, tight, black leather skirt and put on a matching leather jacket. She pushed her feet into high-heeled black shoes with very pointed toes, smeared pink lipstick across her mouth, ran her fingers through her blonde bouffant and was ready. She never wore knickers. Not when she wasn't working. She said she liked it better without, and who was I to argue?

Tracey chose black underwear too. A see-through bra and a tiny pair of transparent knickers under a T-shirt and snow-washed jeans so tight they needed zips on the bottoms of the legs to allow her to get her bare feet through them, which she then squeezed into white stilettos. Over the whole ensemble she wore a shiny black plastic mac belted at the waist. She slapped on some greasy red lipstick, pouted at herself in the mirror, combed her short yellow hair and she too was ready for whatever the night would bring.

Me? I was wearing jeans of that dangerous age, when one more wash might mean self-destruction, black leather baseball boots, and a white cowboy-style shirt. I took my old leather jacket off the hook behind the door, and I was ready too.

We went downstairs to the street and turned in the direction of their local. It was a big, Victorian pub, close to Wandsworth prison, called the Halfway House. Once upon a time it must have had as many as half a dozen bars, but now it just had two: a big saloon bar and an even bigger public bar, with three pool tables, a permanent karaoke set-up, and a DJ's booth perched in one corner between massive speakers and a chrome scaffold that supported a full light show.

It was only just after opening time when we arrived and the place was pretty well deserted.

We went into the saloon, and Tracey and Dawn went over to a table whilst I scared up a round of drinks. Between seven and nine on a Sunday was euphemistically called 'Happy Hour', so I had to wait whilst the barman made up a Long Island iced tea and a Pink Lady. I ordered a pint of lager to keep me company while he mixed them.

'How's it going?' he asked as he did the business.

Do you know, I couldn't remember?

'Can't complain,' I said. My voice sounded strange, and I couldn't remember when I'd last spoken either.

'Not much point if you do,' he said.

I had a horrible feeling we were going to get into cliché hell.

'Too true,' I said, and lit a cigarette.

'Still, could be worse,' he said.

I nodded.

He put the first of the cocktails up on the bar. 'You seem to be doing all right for yourself.' He looked over in obvious admiration at my companions.

I nodded again.

'Lovely girls,' he said. 'I caught their show the other week at the Sportsman.'

'Did you now?' I said.

'Yes,' he replied. 'I've always been a great admirer of the naked female form myself.'

He was about five foot two, maybe fifty-five, maybe a little older, with thin dark hair going grey at the edges, the kind of face a weasel would consider distinguished, and he spoke with a slight Irish lilt to his voice.

'Did you enjoy it?' I asked, as he deftly prepared the Pink Lady.

'Marvellous stuff. Marvellous stuff.' Suddenly he realised that he might be stepping on a few corns. 'No offence meant of course, sir.'

'None taken,' I said. 'I've always been a great admirer of the naked female form myself.'

He smiled in relief. 'That's all right then. As long as you didn't mind me saying so. Of course I've nothing but the greatest respect for Dawn and Tracey. A pair of real ladies I always say.'

'That's good,' I said. 'I'm glad you always say that. I always say that myself. It's always gratifying to find someone who agrees with me about so much.'

He put the second cocktail next to the first and totted up the bill. I paid him with a tenner, and got about enough change to keep my car on a parking meter for half an hour.

He looked at the few coins on the bar sadly and said, 'Sure, the cost of living's going up all the time, isn't it?'

I pushed them back over to him and said, 'Have one on me.'

His face lit up like a sunrise and the coins vanished into his pocket quicker than it takes to tell.

'Thank you very kindly,' he said. 'And have a splendid evening.' He looked wistfully over at Tracey and Dawn.

'Thank *you*,' I replied. 'I intend to.' And I picked up the drinks and took them over to the table.

'He took his time, didn't he?' complained Tracey when I arrived.

'If you must drink things like this, what do you expect?' I said.

Dawn looked over at the bar where the barman was still gazing in our direction.

'He's a filthy little bugger, him,' she said. 'He comes creeping round to see us on his day off. Sits right up the front, and he never even blinks in case he might miss something.'

She stuck her finger into Tracey's Pink Lady, and licked the sticky mess off whilst looking straight at the barman.

His eyes widened, and after a few seconds he went to see if anyone wanted serving in the other bar.

Tracey and Dawn giggled.

'He's chicken, though,' said Tracey. 'He only looks, don't do nothing else.'

'I know,' said Dawn. 'I met him down the butcher's the other day and asked him to show me his meat. He went bright red and ran away.'

'Didn't he say nothing?' asked Tracey.

'No. I expect he was saving his breath for when he got home and blew up his rubber girlfriend.'

Their giggles turned to gales of laughter at that example of Dawn's wit, and I began to feel a bit sorry for the poor bloke. Once these two got you in their sights you were a dead man.

'So where we gonna eat, Nick?' asked Dawn, after their laughter subsided.

'You want Chinese don't you?' I said.

'That's favourite,' she replied.

'Let's go to the Peking Inn then,' I said.

'Great,' said Tracey. 'Can we have the duck?'

'Have whatever you like, love,' I replied.

'T'riffic,' she said.

We sat and finished our drinks, and I went up for another round. The little barman avoided me and I got served by the guv'nor of the boozer.

'How's tricks?' he asked.

Here we go again, I thought.

'Not too bad,' I said.

'Ask young Dawn to pop over, will you? – Nick, isn't it?'

I agreed that it was.

'There's a bit of a do on next week. Local football club. They want a bit of entertainment.'

And a bit is probably what they'll get with that pair, I thought.

'Good money,' he said, putting the cocktails on the bar with a wink. 'Great bunch of lads in the team.'

'I'll tell her,' I said, as I picked up the glasses and went back to the table.

'Guv'nor wants you,' I said to Dawn as I sat down. 'Got a bit of extra work.'

'Great,' she said, looked over to the bar, and waved at the landlord.

'Football team,' I explained.

'T'riffic,' said Tracey.

I had to admit these girls were gluttons for punishment.

Dawn took a sip from her glass and got up and wiggled over the carpet towards the bar. I watched as she went, as did every other member of the largely male clientele who had started to fill the place. I couldn't blame them. Under the tight leather of her skirt, the movement of her buttocks was sheer poetry.

When I looked back, Tracey gave me a big smile round the edge of *her* glass. 'Enjoying yourself, Nick?' she asked.

She was a kind soul was Trace. A bit dense, but kind nevertheless.

Dawn came back with the details of the engagement and sat down, showing off a lot of stocking top and bare thigh which got a fair amount of comment from the punters.

'Cheeky buggers,' she said, and I had to smile. What else did she expect?

I finished my second pint of lager and looked at the sticky dregs of their drinks. 'We off then?'

We left the place to a few more comments in their direction. They flounced out like they felt insulted, but I knew that they loved it. It was when the comments stopped that they'd have to worry.

We walked down to East Hill where the restaurant was and, it still being comparatively early, got a table with no bother.

The waiters knew Tracey and Dawn well, and brought out the

prawn crackers and Liebfraumilch without being asked. How those two could sit and drink Liebfraumilch I'd never know.

I asked for a bottle of Tiger beer, and had a quick squint at the menu.

We settled for prawn and crab meat soup for three, half a crispy duck with all the trimmings, sweet and sour prawns, noodles with three kinds of meat, bang bang chicken, deep-fried beef in chilli and green peppers, and double egg-fried rice.

The food was good, the service quick, without the waiters actually snatching the chopsticks out of your mouth, and the toffee apples for dessert were extremely sweet and sticky. We all finished with Irish coffees and as the town hall clock struck ten we were back on the street and heading home.

When we got back to the flat, Dawn broke out the Southern Comfort and lemonade, rolled another giant spliff, and we settled down on the sofa in front of the late film on BBC2. I had Tracey on one side of me and Dawn on the other like a pair of book-ends, and I was certainly feeling very little pain by the time the movie ended.

Tracey was fast asleep by then, and Dawn and I were getting pretty sweet and sticky ourselves, so we left her and moved into the bedroom.

And that was more or less that for the rest of the night.

3

So that's the way it was that morning. Just another morning as far as I was concerned. Until the telephone rang and everything changed, just like it always seems to.

I leant over and picked up the receiver. 'Yeah?' I said.

'Mr Sharman?' I didn't recognise the voice.

'Yeah,' I said again.

'It's Frank Grant here.'

I didn't recognise the name either. 'Yeah,' I said for the third time.

There was a long pause as if the name alone should have meant something to me. 'Frank Grant. You remember.'

'No.' I didn't even bother to think about it.

'Frank Grant,' he repeated, almost like a mantra. Or as if maybe it was the last thing in the world that he was sure of.

I was getting tired of guessing games. 'Listen, Frank Grant,' I said, 'I've got a lousy hangover and I'm tired. I'm sure I should know you, but I don't. So give me a clue, or get lost.'

'You used to call me "Sailor" Grant.'

And that's when I dropped the phone. It bounced off my chest, and I grabbed for it, catching it before it hit the carpet.

'*Sailor Grant*,' I said.

'That's right. Do you remember now?'

I would have thought it was bloody obvious that I did.

'Yes,' I replied. 'How did you get this number?'

'I asked around. You haven't moved far.'

I had, but I came back.

'Where are you?' I asked.

'Close.'

That was what I was afraid of.

'It's been a long time,' I said.

'Twelve years I've been inside. I'm out now on licence.'

Twelve years, I thought. Could it really be that long? Longer really, what with the trial and all. But of course it could. Where did it all go?

'What do you want?' I asked.

'I want to see you.'

Dream on, I thought.

'I don't think so,' I said.

'You know I didn't do it, Mr Sharman. You were the only one who believed me.'

I didn't want to remember.

Another pause lengthened down the telephone line as he waited for a reply.

When I didn't make one, he spoke again. Pleading this time.

'Please, Mr Sharman. It isn't too late to put it right. I need to see you.'

'No, Sailor,' I said. 'Perhaps you do, but I really don't want to see *you*. It was all too long ago.'

'*Please*, Mr Sharman.' He was sounding desperate by then.

'Not in this life, son,' I said, put down the phone, and reached over and pulled the plug out of the wall. I took another mouthful of beer, laid my head back on a cushion, and let my mind float back twelve years.

4

Detective Constable Sharman. First day attached to CID at Brixton nick with the new rank, on transfer from Kennington. Mid-twenties with his whole life in front of him. The sky was the limit. Who knew where he might end up? Commissioner maybe.

It was not to be, of course. DC was the highest rank I ever attained. But then. Oh, then.

Young. Fit. Newly married. First mortgage on a flat in Streatham, and a baby soon. My wife just had *that* feeling. In love forever, with no one else but her. But forever is a very long time.

I was driving a second-hand Cortina then. One careful lady owner who only used it on Sunday to drive to church. You know the deal. 'You're a police officer, sir?' said the salesman. 'Our favourite kind of customer. Of *course* we'll come down a couple of hundred quid on the asking price. A free service and a tankful of petrol? No problem. And listen. If you hear of any nice motors coming up for auction through the Met, let us know. We'll make sure you don't lose by it.'

That's how it starts. And you end up taking backhanders for looking the other way, and eventually commit grand larceny.

But that morning, all of that was yet to come.

I arrived at eight-thirty sharp. New suit. Clean white shirt neatly ironed by the loving wife. Tie done up tight, and black lace-up shoes polished brightly.

I reported to the detective inspector. He seemed about as interested in me as I was in nuclear physics, and sent me to introduce myself to the detective sergeant. If anything he was even less interested, and told me to go to the canteen to find another DC to talk to. He was eating double egg, sausage, beans, tinned tomatoes, chips and a fried slice. If anything he was the least interested of the lot. He sneered at my suit and made me buy him a cup of tea.

When he'd finished his breakfast, he looked at his watch. 'I'll show you round the manor when I've had my tea,' he said. 'I know a boozer that needs checking out. Guv'nor should be bottling up in a few minutes. He'll be glad to buy us a pint or two.'

The DC took out an unmarked car that stank of last night's Chinese takeout, and we drove through the back streets of Brixton to a little pub close to a council estate. The draymen were delivering, and we walked round the back, through a door and into the saloon bar. There was a dour-looking geezer behind the bar, leaning on the counter drinking a cup of coffee. As soon as he saw us he took down two pint glasses. 'Lenny,' he said, by way of greeting.

The DC's name was Leonard Millar, with an 'a'.

'Tom,' said Lenny. 'This fashion plate is Nick Sharman. Detective constable of this parish. He's the replacement for Sammy Plant. You'll be seeing something of him over the foreseeable future, I have no doubt.'

'A pleasure,' said Tom, and stuck out his mitten.

I took it and shook it, and agreed that indeed it was a pleasure.

'What's your poison, Nick? Don't mind if I call you that?' said Tom.

'No,' I replied. 'A pint of lager would be good.'

I wasn't *that* used to drinking so early, but I'd soon learn.

Tom pulled two pints, and Lenny and I dragged a pair of stools up to the bar. Lenny said, 'What kind of weekend did you have, Tom?'

'Quiet,' replied Tom.

'Anything known about that blag at Safeways last week?'

'Not a word, Lenny.'

'If you hear anything – no matter what.'

'You'll be the first to know.'

'Good,' said Lenny, and turned to me. He was about thirty-five. Going to seed fast. Too many early-morning fry-ups, followed by a few pints probably. He was shorter than me, and fat, with a chin that almost hid the knot of his greasy tie. 'Got any fags, Nick?' he asked.

I took out a packet of Silk Cut and put them on the bar. They helped themselves. I took one myself, and Tom lit all three with an ancient Ronson petrol lighter.

Just then the draymen came in, and Tom busied himself pulling them a pint of best bitter each. Lenny sank half his lager with one swallow and said, 'Good bloke, Tom. Well worth cultivating. Knows a lot of what goes on round here. Treat him right and he'll do the same to you. This place never closes.'

'Don't the punters know he's on our side?'

'They know we come in here. But if the punters stayed out of every pub in Brixton that makes us welcome, most would have been out of business years ago. No. It's a game, Nick. You must know that. You've been in the job long enough. We protect our sources, and they protect us. We don't take liberties. Nothing's ever said. If the info doesn't pan out, we don't come back with baseball bats. That's not the way it works. Learn that, and you'll not go far wrong.'

The pair of us sat in the bar until opening time, and through till the three o'clock bell went, and Lenny told me something about the DS and the DI I'd be working with. I was getting well pissed by then, and hadn't had to put my hand in my pocket once. I was beginning to wonder when we'd do some real work, when Lenny said, 'Time-to-go time, son. Don't think it's going to be like this every day. The DS told me to break you in gentle. I think we'll get back to the factory and see what's occurred whilst we've been enjoying a nice drink in here.'

'Suits me,' I said.

'You drive,' said Lenny. 'You're more pissed than me.'

So I did.

5

When we got back to the station, the balloon had gone up. A balloon that wouldn't land again for another twelve years or more.

The DI was standing in the CID office, with the DS who'd sent me to see Lenny Millar. The inspector's name was Paul Grisham. The sergeant's, Collier. Terry Collier.

'Where have you two been?' demanded Grisham.

'I've been showing Sharman round the plot,' said Lenny.

'Round the pubs more like,' replied Grisham. 'Sharman, you look pissed.' He wasn't a detective inspector for nothing.

'A girl's been raped,' Grisham went on. 'Behind some lockup garages at the back of the town hall. It's a bad one. She's been pretty badly knocked about.'

'How badly?' asked Lenny.

'Badly enough. She's still unconscious. They don't know if she'll live.'

'When?' asked Lenny.

'An hour or so ago. When you were on your fifth pint.'

I was beginning to wonder if the man had us bugged.

'Do we know who she was?' Lenny again.

'No. Not yet. I've got two DCs and the uniforms out searching the area to see what they can find. She had no ID on her.'

'No bag?' I asked.

Grisham's eyes moved to me. 'Oh, it speaks,' he said. 'No. No bag.'

'Anyone in the frame?' asked Lenny.

'No,' Grisham said. 'Not yet.'

Collier got into the act. 'You two,' he said to Lenny and me, 'get out and have a drive round. See if you can find anyone who fits the bill. And stay out of the pubs.'

'Yes, skip,' said Lenny, and the phone rang.

Grisham picked it up, barked his name into the receiver and listened. 'Christ,' he said. 'Are you sure?'

He listened again.

'Has anybody told him?'

He was silent for another moment.

'Jesus,' he said. 'Why on our ground? OK. I'll make sure he's informed.'

He put down the phone, and stood for a moment, before turning to face the three of us again.

'The girl who was raped. She's been identified. Her name's Carol Harvey.'

No one said a word.

'She's the daughter of a certain DI Harvey who's stationed down in Purley. And if that's not bad enough, she's also the niece of our own dear detective superintendent, Alan Byrne. And she's only fourteen, poor cow.'

'Christ!' said Collier. 'Are you sure?'

'Yes I am,' replied Grisham. 'Her face is pretty well knocked about, but one of the WPCs down at the hospital recognised her. She's been here to see her uncle a few times.'

'And Mr Byrne doesn't know?' asked Collier.

'It's my pleasant duty to inform him,' said Grisham.

Then he noticed me and Lenny, still standing there listening.

'What are you two doing?' he shouted. 'You've got a job to do. Get out and do it. I want a result on this yesterday.'

6

Lenny and I went back to the car, and he drove slowly round
Brixton. I was feeling lousy, and wanted another drink, but I
knew that would have to wait.

He spotted Sailor Grant outside a fish shop, eating chips out of a
bag.

'Sailor,' said Lenny.

'Who?'

'The little shithead there, eating his supper.'

I looked at the man that Lenny had pointed out. He was about
thirty-five. Short, thin, and shifty looking. His hair was blond and
lank and lay close to his head. His face was as vacant as an empty
shop. He was wearing jeans a size too big, and a jacket a size too
small.

Lovely, I thought. As upstanding a citizen as I'd seen in a long
time. This geezer was a pull waiting to happen, and we were ready
to oblige.

'Who is he?' I asked.

'Sailor Grant. Used to be in the Merchant Navy till they threw
him out for conduct unbecoming. A right nasty little scrote.'

'What does he do?'

'Takes his cock out in front of little kids mostly. Hangs around
the schools. You know the type. He's scared to show it to a grown

woman in case she'd tear it off and stuff it down his throat. I've nicked him half a dozen times myself.'

'Does he do more than flash?'

'Not so far. But there's always a first time.'

'Carol Harvey'd be a bit old for him, wouldn't she? If he's into young kids. Nonces are like leopards, they rarely change their spots.'

'She's only fourteen, Grisham said. And we don't know how big she is. She might be right up Sailor's alley. Or maybe he thought it was time to progress to bigger and better things.'

By then, Sailor had turned and was walking along the road, still eating his chips, and we were shadowing him on the other side of the road. He didn't seem to be in any hurry to get anywhere.

'Gonna give him a tug?' I asked.

'Sure we are.'

Lenny waited for a gap in the traffic and steered the car across the road, and let down his window. 'Hello, Sailor,' he said, and the way he said it didn't sound in the least bit funny. 'Got a chip for me?'

Sailor Grant almost dropped the greasy package he was holding.

'Hello, Mr Millar,' he said. 'What can I do for you?'

'You been a naughty boy again?'

Sailor's face went white, and I could see that he was trembling at the question and the tone in which it had been put.

'No, guv. Honest.'

'You haven't got an honest bone in your body,' said Lenny.

He stopped the car and got out. He took the bag of chips from Sailor's hand, and dropped them into an overflowing litter bin where a few slid out of their container, and joined the rest of the rubbish on the pavement.

'Get in,' said Lenny. 'We'll give you a lift.'

'It's all right, guv. I can walk, honest.'

Lenny grabbed him by the upper arm, opened the back door of the car, thrust Sailor into the back seat, and slid in after him. 'You drive, Nick,' he said. 'I'll keep our friend company in the back here. By the way, Sailor, this is DC Sharman. Remember his face. It's for sure he'll remember yours.'

I moved over to the driving seat, put the car into gear and pulled away.

'Where to?' I asked.

'Just drive.'

This was all years before the Police and Criminal Evidence Act. We often used to conduct interviews in the car then. All the better to get a cough from the suspect.

'Where were you earlier this afternoon?' asked Lenny.

'About.'

'About where?'

'Just about.'

'Who with?'

'By myself.'

'Sailor doesn't have many friends,' said Lenny to the back of my head. 'Do you, Sailor?' he said to our prisoner, if you could call him that.

'I've got friends.'

'Are they all horrible little nonces like you? Or do you count the little kids you frighten with your willy?'

Sailor didn't reply.

'A young girl was raped earlier today,' said Lenny. 'Round the back of the town hall. Did you get up that way at all this afternoon, Sailor?'

'No. Honest. I was on the other side.'

'The other side of what?'

'Brixton. I was up Stockwell way.'

'Handy that,' said Lenny.

I pulled the car into the kerb, set the handbrake, and turned to face the back of the car.

'Did you touch the girl?' I asked.

'I don't know no girl,' said Sailor, happy to talk to a new face who might be on his side.

'We'll get a doctor to examine your privates,' I said. 'He'll be able to tell.'

'I had a bath. I'm clean.'

'You don't know the meaning of the word,' said Lenny.

'When?' I asked.

'What?' said Sailor.

'When did you have a bath?'

'This morning.'

'Are you sure?' said Lenny. 'Sure it wasn't this afternoon, after you screwed her?'

'No.'

'Have you been wearing those clothes all day?' I asked.

'Yeah.'

'We'll search where you live,' I said. 'And examine all your clothes. If you're lying…'

'I'm not. I ain't got that many clothes. The rest's in the laundry.'

'When did you put them in?' I asked.

'Just now –' Sailor stopped as the enormity of what he'd said hit him.

'A bath and clean clothes all in one day,' said Lenny. 'Is it your birthday, or what?'

'Me clothes were dirty.'

'I bet they were,' said Lenny. 'Covered in come stains. Was that it?'

'No. Just dirty.'

'Are they in the machine now?' I asked.

'Yeah. I was going to have my chips and go back and get them.'

'We'll get them for you,' I said. 'On the way to the station.'

'No,' protested Sailor. 'Not the nick.'

'It's got to be,' I said. 'Right, Lenny?'

'That's the way it looks to me. You're in dead trouble here, Sailor. The girl was a copper's daughter, and our super's niece.'

Sailor went even paler, as Lenny spoke.

'I never…' he said, but we weren't listening. I put the car into a U-turn, and headed back to the laundry next to the chip shop. Lenny Millar and Sailor came in with me, and I emptied the machine he'd been using, put his clean clothes into the black plastic sack he'd brought them in, and drove them, him and Lenny to the station.

Lenny and I wheeled Sailor Grant into an interview room at five in the afternoon. We'd called in on the RT and Collier and Grisham were waiting for us. We had our suspect in for questioning, and the fun was just about to begin.

7

'Good work, boys,' said Grisham.

I didn't know what was particularly good about it. We'd driven round for ten minutes and picked up some poor unfortunate bastard who couldn't cope with life. Big deal. The streets of London were full of them. The fact that this *particular* one got his rocks off showing his penis to children had little to do with it. What was important was that the tidal wave of officialdom had gathered, and was ready to break upon the beach. Someone from the family of two senior policemen had been interfered with. We needed a body. Any body. And we'd got one.

'Let's have a few words with him,' said Grisham. 'Lenny. Terry. You come in with me. Sharman. You still look lousy. Go and get some tea.'

It was a pleasure. 'Yes, guv,' I said, and made for the canteen.

'And bring back four cups for us when you're done.'

'Yes, guv,' I said again.

I had a cup of tea, sitting all alone at a table in the corner. The few uniforms who were taking a refreshment break knew what had happened, and were clocking me surreptitiously. Finally, one big constable came over to my table and stood looking at me.

'Yes?' I said, looking up at him.

He stuck out his hand. 'My name's Dave. Dave Conroy. You're new.'

I agreed that I was, took his hand and told him who I was.

'Welcome aboard,' he said. 'I was on the shout for that girl who was raped. Byrne's niece. I hear you've got someone.'

I nodded.

'Who?'

'Sailor Grant,' I replied. 'I believe he's well-known round here.'

The uniform nodded grimly. 'I know him,' he said. 'Looks like he's moved into the big league.'

'He'll be out on the streets again in an hour,' I said. 'He's not our man.'

'What makes you say that?'

I shrugged. 'Dunno,' I said. 'Intuition.'

The uniform nodded. 'I hope you're wrong,' he said. 'Our lives are going to be miserable until we catch the sod who *did* do it.'

'That's what worries me,' I said. 'We're jumping to too many conclusions for my liking.'

Conroy nodded. 'I'd better be going. Plenty still to do.'

'I reckon he's still out there,' I said.

Conroy went back to his mates to report on the conversation. They kept glancing in my direction as they finished their teas and left.

I finished mine a few minutes later, got four more cups and a sugar bowl for Grisham and Co, and went back down to the interview room.

I took the teas in and put them on the table. Grant was sitting in a chair behind it. The three police officers were standing round him.

Collier grabbed my arm, and steered me out of the room. 'I hear you don't like our friend for this,' he said.

I shrugged. Christ, but that was fast. My new friend PC Conroy must have had a quick word with Collier.

'Well, do you or don't you?'

'Not really.'

'And of course you'd fucking know. An officer of your vast experience.'

'It's just an opinion.'

'Well, Sharman, in future keep your fucking opinions to yourself, until you're asked. Understand?'

'Yes.'

'Yes, *what*?'

'Yes, sir.'

'Right. You get off home to your wife now. We don't want you on overtime on your first day, do we?'

'No, sir.'

'Very good. Report to me in the morning.'

'Yes, sir.'

He turned on his heel and went back into the interview room, and shut the door in my face.

So I did as he suggested, and went home to my wife.

8

When I got into the nick the next morning and presented myself for duty in the CID office, Collier was there on his own. 'Any luck with Grant?' I asked.

'No. He won't budge.' I could tell he wasn't in the best of moods about it. Or me.

'What's on the agenda for today?' I asked.

He looked at me nastily. 'For *us*, continued investigations and interrogations of the suspect on the Harvey rape. For *you*, some follow-up calls that your predecessor didn't get round to. Get a motor and get on to them.' He tossed me a file, yay thick. 'Hope you've got an *A-Z*. You'll need one.'

I think he just wanted me and my opinions out of the way. I played it by the book. 'Right you are, skip,' I said. 'I'll check in later.'

'Do that.' And he walked out of the room.

I spent the morning trying to track down various witnesses to crime, and victims of it. Most seemed either to be at work or to have vanished off the face of the earth. It was not a productive few hours. I lunched at a greasy spoon, and then popped in for a drink at Tom's pub, half hoping that Lenny might be there, for someone to talk to.

He wasn't. But Tom greeted me like a long-lost friend and stuck me up a gratis pint of lager straight off.

'Terrible thing what happened,' he said.

'What's that?' I asked.

'Your super's niece. It was in the paper this morning.'

'Right,' I agreed.

'I see you got someone.'

'Someone,' I said. 'But not the geezer who did it. At least *I* don't think so.' I wondered how long that would take to be reported to Collier. Who the fuck cared?

'Why's that?' asked Tom.

'Don't know. That's why I'm here, and not back at the station, talking to the man concerned. I think my DS reckons I'm rocking the boat.'

'Are you?'

'Don't think so. Can I use your phone?'

He took it from off the back of the bar and put it on the counter in front of me, then vanished. I could see why his pub was so popular. I dialled the number of the nick and asked to be put through to CID.

'CID. Millar,' said a voice.

'Lenny. It's Nick Sharman.'

'Mr Unpopular. Where are you?'

'Tom's.'

'You learn fast. How's it going?'

'A total wash. Nobody on my list's about.'

'That's Collier's special shit list. He only gives it to you when he wants you out of the way.'

'How's it going with that?'

'Another total wash. I'm beginning to think you were right. Sailor's even beginning to convince me. We'll probably kick him out later.'

'Any other face in the frame?'

'Not really. The usual collection of losers who get a hard-on pinching knickers off lines or peeping into someone's back bedroom.'

'That's bad.'

'You can say that again. All the real perverts round here seem to be visiting Her Majesty at the moment.'

'What shall I do?'

'Stay at Tom's and have another drink. I wish I was with you. Come in later. Collier won't even notice.'

So that's what I did. I had another pint or two, made some back calls – where by a miracle I managed to interview a couple of people, without any conspicuous result – and wandered into the nick about four.

Collier was standing in the general office behind the reception area. 'Sharman,' he said. 'Any luck with that lot of calls I gave you?'

'Not really. I managed to dig a couple out of their pits. I'll write it up.'

'Harvey's here.'

'The DI? Carol Harvey's father?'

'The same. He wants to see you.'

'Why?'

''Cos you were there when Grant was nicked.'

'Any luck with him?' I asked.

Collier shook his head.

We went upstairs, and a large, dark-haired man was coming out of Superintendent Byrne's office. With him was a young girl of about twelve. She had long, thick red hair, wore Coke-bottle-bottom glasses and a school uniform. Both she and her father looked like they'd had better days. I imagine they had.

'This is Sharman, sir,' said Collier. 'Sharman, DI Harvey.'

'Oh, Sharman. Good, I'd like a word. Jackie, will you stay with Sergeant Collier? I want to speak to the DC in private. Then we'll go up to the hospital.'

'Come with me, love,' said Collier. 'I'll find you a cup of tea and somewhere to sit. That office is empty, sir. Use that.' He gestured at a door beside us.

The girl looked at her father, then me, then Collier, shrugged, and went with him in the direction of the canteen.

Harvey opened the office door and led me in. He perched on the edge of the desk and I stood.

'This is a dreadful thing,' he said.

I nodded.

'Do you think this bloke Grant did it?'

I shook my head.

'Why not?'

Everybody kept asking me that. 'Not his style, Mr Harvey,' I said. 'He hasn't got the guts to touch. Looking's his thing. Looking and showing. That's how he's got his kicks up until now.'

'Why'd you pull him then?'

'It wasn't my idea. I'm new here. DC Millar's nicked him before. He was about. Then there's the business of the bath and all his clothes being in the wash. He fits the bill.'

'He could have changed his MO,' said Harvey.

'He could,' I agreed. 'Maybe I'm wrong.'

'I've spoken to Millar. He still likes him for it.'

That's not what he said on the phone, I thought. He's humouring you, my son.

'Have you spoken to Grant?' asked Harvey.

'Briefly.'

Harvey crashed one fist into the palm of his other hand. When he looked at me I saw he was close to tears. 'My daughter,' he said. 'Why?'

'I'm sorry,' I replied, and it sounded pretty lame. 'We're still looking. We'll find him eventually.'

'You married, Sharman?'

'Yes.'

'Kids?'

'My wife thinks there might be one on the way. We've only been married a little while.'

'I hope for your sake it's a boy.'

She wasn't as a matter of fact, and I'm not a little bit sorry. Not so far.

We stayed in the office talking for another five or ten minutes, then Harvey looked at his watch, and I knew the interview was over.

'Just keep at it, son,' he said. 'Don't stop until you get the bastard who did it. Whoever it is.'

'I won't, sir. And nor will any other officer at this station. Count on it.'

'I believe you,' he said. 'And I will.'

He shook my hand too hard and we left the office.

As we went into the corridor, Collier and Harvey's daughter came out of the super's office. Collier looked serious and Jackie Harvey's glasses were smeared.

'Just saying goodbye to her uncle,' Collier said quickly.

The girl peered at me through the thick lenses she wore, and her eyes were very old.

'Come along, Jackie,' said Harvey. 'Let's go and see how your sister is.'

Collier and I watched as they turned the corner of the corridor. Jackie Harvey looked back, and the expression on her face chilled me to the bone.

9

'Come on then, Sharman,' said Collier. 'Don't hang about. Let's go and see Mr Grant. I think it's about time we got him to tell us the truth about what happened yesterday.'

'I thought it was a washout, skip,' I said. 'I thought you were going to let him go.'

Collier turned on me furiously. 'Who told you that? DI Grisham and I say when he goes. Don't pay any attention to rumours amongst the lower ranks. Grant did it. I know he did. And now he's going to tell us all about it.'

'Can we hold him much longer without charging him?' I asked.

'We *are* going to charge him. No, you were there, *you're* going to charge him. Any problems with that?'

Lots, I thought.

'No, sir,' I said. 'No problems at all.'

So we went downstairs and I charged Sailor Grant with the assault and rape of Carol Harvey.

'Do you want a solicitor present?' I asked after the formal charges had been made.

Grant shook his head.

Then the interrogation began.

In those days we didn't tape-record interviews. All that was to come later. So were DNA tests. All that had happened was, at some point the previous evening, Grant had given some blood. His group was the most common. So was the blood group of whoever had raped Carol Harvey.

Having that blood group was definitely the unluckiest thing that had ever happened to Sailor Grant.

I was left alone with him for a few minutes whilst Collier went and fetched Grisham and Lenny Millar.

'I never done it, Mr Sharman,' he said pleadingly. 'Honest, I never done it. I couldn't hurt anyone. Not like that.'

'We think you did, Sailor,' I said.

I still didn't, but I had to stand solidly with my superiors.

'I couldn't,' he insisted. 'I never have.'

'What?' I asked.

He wouldn't answer at first, just squirmed around on his seat.

I moved my chair round and put my hand on his shoulder. 'Tell me, Sailor,' I said. 'Tell me. It might help.'

'I've never…' He refused to finish.

I sat silently, my hand still resting lightly on his shoulder.

'Oh Christ,' he said, squeezing the words out through clenched teeth. 'I've never done it with anyone.'

'Done what?' Although I had a good idea by then. I just wanted him to tell me himself.

'I've never done that.' He paused. 'Been with a woman.' And the tears came.

'Never?' I said. 'Not when you were in the navy?'

'No.'

'Why not?'

He didn't answer at first.

I didn't speak either.

'I'm scared of them,' he said.

Who isn't? I thought.

'That's nothing to be ashamed of,' I said.

'That's why I do what I do. Show me willie to kids.'

'Because you're a virgin?' I asked.

He nodded his reply, and Grisham, Collier and Lenny Millar came into the interview room.

'Talk to you, guv,' I said to Grisham. 'Outside.'

Grisham and Collier went back into the corridor, and I joined them. Lenny stayed with Grant.

'He says he couldn't have done it,' I said.

'Bollocks,' said Collier.

'Why?' asked Grisham.

'Because he never has,' I said.

'What?' demanded Collier.

I knew I was digging myself deeper into the mire with every word. 'Had a woman,' I said.

'Fuck off,' said Collier. 'You believe that shit?'

'I think so,' I said. 'He's terrified of women. That's why he shows his dick to children. It was like Lenny said yesterday when we nicked him. He's terrified of anyone past primary school age.'

'*Bollocks.*' This time Collier shouted the word, and I could see a vein ticking in his forehead. 'Sharman, I'm beginning to lose patience with you. I told you yesterday to keep your opinions to yourself until asked.'

'I talked to the prisoner,' I said. 'It's my duty to report what was said to a senior officer.'

At that I thought Collier was going to self-destruct.

'*Your duty,*' he said, 'your fucking duty is to do what DI Grisham and I tell you. And we tell you he's as guilty as sin. I don't care if he'd never fucked anyone until yesterday afternoon. Because even if he hadn't, he did then. He lost his cherry with Carol Harvey, boy. It's a fact, I'm telling you. Now get inside that room, and we'll get to the bottom of all this.'

The next few hours were the worst I'd ever known in the job. Up until then, I suppose *I'd* been a virgin. A virgin as to what could go on behind closed doors in a police station.

I lost my cherry too that night. And like everyone else in that stinking little room, I would never be the same again.

Grisham, Collier and Millar took turns at interrogating Grant. They never let up. I wasn't asked to speak. Just sit and listen.

Grant himself was terrified. So terrified he kept changing what he'd said about his movements the previous day, and why he'd made them. He contradicted himself on every detail except one. That he hadn't attacked Carol Harvey.

We took a break about ten.

We left a uniform with Grant, and sloped off to the pub opposite for a livener. It was my round. Both times.

'He won't shift,' said Grisham to Collier. Somehow it seemed as if the junior officer had taken charge of the case and the DI was deferring to him.

I didn't get it.

'He'll fucking well shift if I say he'll shift,' said Collier, and I knew that things were beginning to go from bad to worse.

'What do you mean?' asked Grisham.

'What I say. Give me and Lenny some time with him on our own.' Then he looked at me. 'And our friend here. I want to teach him some of the tricks of the trade.'

'All right,' said Grisham. 'I've got some things to do. I'll catch you later.'

'Don't leave it too long, Paul. We wouldn't want you to miss all the fun, would we?' said Collier, and I didn't like the way he said it.

Grisham looked almost as bad as I felt, as he left the boozer.

The three of us, Lenny, Collier and I, were back in the nick by eleven. We dismissed the young uniformed constable who was looking after Grant, and the shit really hit the fan.

Collier and Lenny took off their coats and ties and hung them neatly over the backs of two chairs.

They were good, I'll say that for them. They didn't mark Sailor up much. Not until the end when it all got too much for me to bear.

And *still* the little bastard wouldn't change his story.

They used towels soaked in water and wrapped round their fists. That way the bruises don't show as much. They stripped Sailor to the waist and took turns beating on his skinny little torso. The slap, slap, slap of wet material on wet skin, and Sailor's cries of pain, and the sound of Lenny's and Collier's grunts of breath, filled the little room until I thought the walls were going to burst.

And Sailor still maintained that he was innocent.

They'd hit him, then take a break and smoke a cigarette and chat together as if nothing was happening, and Sailor would perch on the edge of his chair and look pleadingly at me.

And what was I doing through all this?

Fuck all, was what I was doing.

I didn't join in, but I didn't try and stop them.

And then Collier lost his temper, and the claret began to flow.

He started slapping Grant around the face. Hard slaps that brought the blood to the surface of his pallid skin.

'Tell me, Sailor,' he said. 'Just tell me that you did it, and this'll stop and we can all get to our beds.'

Sailor looked down at the floor and shook his head and Collier planted a punch on the side of his jaw that knocked him off his seat, and left him lying on the floor spitting out a tooth in a mouthful of blood and saliva.

Lenny Millar pulled him to his feet, stood beside him and trapped his arms, and Collier punched Sailor again between the eyes.

'No,' I said. 'Stop. You'll kill the fucker.' And I grabbed Collier's arm.

He shook it off and turned on me and said, 'If you don't like it, get out.'

Which is exactly what I did. I got out and went into the lavatory, and put my head against the cool tiles that covered the walls, and wondered if I'd chosen the correct career.

I took a piss, washed my hands and looked into the mirror over the washbasin. It was still me in the reflection. But I knew that from that night onwards I would never feel the same about the man I saw in the mirror.

10

I stayed in the washroom for another fifteen minutes and smoked two cigarettes. When I went back to the interview room, Sailor Grant had gone. Collier and Lenny were sitting in their two chairs drinking more tea. DI Grisham was perched on the edge of the table, also drinking tea.

'Where is he?' I asked.

'He had a nasty fall on the stairs,' said Collier. 'You should know, you saw it. We all did, didn't we?'

Lenny and Grisham nodded. I looked at Grisham. He wouldn't catch my eye. I wondered how *he* was going to feel about mirrors for a while. I was finding it harder and harder to believe that an officer of his rank was going along with all this.

'We've called for the surgeon,' said Collier. 'He should be here soon. No problem.'

Collier stood up and picked a statement form off the table and slapped me in the chest with it.

'Grant's confession to the rape of Carol Harvey yesterday. I told you it would be only a matter of time before he coughed.' He lowered his voice so that only I could hear. 'And I told him, and I'm telling you, *anyone*, anyone at all, that goes against what I say happened here today is going to regret it. Do I make myself clear?'

'Are you threatening me?' I asked.

'Don't be fucking stupid. Just look around. We're the ones who say if you get on in this job or not. Play the game and you will. Don't and you won't.'

And he smiled a nasty smile and raised his voice and said, 'Who's coming for a celebration? We've had a result and we all deserve a good drink. I know a place that's still open.'

And though I hated myself for it, I went.

Carol Harvey died later that night without regaining consciousness. The doctors said it was a miracle that she'd lived as long as she did after her brutal attacker had left her for dead.

The next morning I charged Sailor Grant with murder. He was in the hospital wing at Brixton prison recovering from the 'nasty fall' he'd had the previous night. He was so sedated that I wondered at the legality of what I was doing. But I was under orders, and in those days I did as I was told. As I finished reading out the charge and again asked if he would like a solicitor present, which again he refused, Sailor reached his skinny hand up from the bed and touched my arm. I looked down at him and he opened his eyes and stared into mine. 'It wasn't me, Mr Sharman,' he croaked. 'As God is my judge.'

I duly noted his remark. It was my job. 'Anything you say may be taken down and given in evidence.' You know the spiel. For all the good it did me, I might as well have saved the ink. But I believed him, and in those few seconds, looking into my eyes, he must have known that I did, to get in touch with me all those years later.

Frank 'Sailor' Grant got a life sentence at the Old Bailey.

Not that it was much of a trial. Sailor pleaded guilty. I think he must have known he was wasting his time doing anything else. He was convicted on his confession alone. There was no forensic evidence at the scene linking him to the crime. Or anyone else for that matter. The trial was all over in a day. Grisham, Collier, Millar, Superintendent Byrne, DI Harvey and I were all in court to see justice being done. Afterwards we got drunk in a bar in the Strand.

I never really fitted into the squad after what happened. I suppose they thought they couldn't trust me. I transferred out of Brixton after a year or so, and didn't return for another three, when I was posted to the drug squad, which eventually was to be my downfall.

By the time I got back, Byrne, Grisham, Collier and Millar had all moved onwards and upwards. They were all fine officers and no doubt were getting exactly what they deserved. But I was glad they weren't at the nick to see me come back. I was still a DC, and my daughter was almost four, and my marriage was disintegrating before my eyes.

There was no doubt in my mind at all that I was getting exactly what *I* deserved.

11

And the earth moved round the sun twelve times, and everyone involved went their appointed ways, until that Monday morning when Sailor Grant called me up on the telephone.

It was almost eleven before I finished remembering, and the contents of the can of beer I was still holding had gone warm.

I thought I'd left that time behind, but deep inside my secret self I had never forgotten Sailor, or how I'd caved in to Collier and his pals that night and afterwards, and I'd carried round a sense of shame ever since.

There was only one thing for it. I rolled a light joint, smoked it, and took myself and my hangover down to the local bar where I got rotten drunk on imported beer and listened to some deep soul music. Not that it's to everyone's taste, but the geezer who was running the place at that time had some tapes of Ruby Johnson, Mable John and Bobby Marchan, which is about as deep soul as you can get without drowning.

When I was on my eighth bottle of Rattlesnake, I called Dawn and Tracey up on the dog.

Tracey answered.

'Fancy a drink?' I said.

'We've been working.'

'What difference does that make?'

That threw her a bit. 'Don't know,' she replied.

'So get down here.'

'Where are you?'

'Guess.'

'Your local.'

'In one.'

'I don't know…'

'I'll spring for the cab.'

That cheered her up. 'Maybe. I'll have to ask Dawn.'

'So ask her.'

The phone went dead as she put her hand over the mouthpiece. 'All right,' she said, when she came back on. 'We'll be there in about an hour.'

'Speed it up then, I'm lonely.'

'All right, Nick, don't get your Y-fronts in a twist.'

'Just get here.'

'Sure. Don't worry. We won't leave you to drink on your own.'

'That's what I like to hear,' I said, and hung up.

I went back to my seat by the bar and the guv'nor had stuck on an Otis Redding tape, and I bought him a beer on the strength of it and sang along quietly to 'My Girl'. But somehow I couldn't get Sailor's telephone call out of my head.

The girls turned up in an antique Ford Consul about four. Somewhere along the way they'd scored a gram of decent coke, so it was straight up into the ladies for a line, which cheered everyone up, and I bought a round of beers and then we shot off for a curry.

Happy days.

They weren't going to last long.

12

Sailor Grant kept phoning. He wouldn't leave it alone.

He was like a man obsessed. In fact he *was* obsessed. And I copped for his obsession at all hours of the day and night.

Eventually, about two weeks after the first call, I gave in.

The phone rang at about seven in the evening.

'Hello,' I said.

'Mr Sharman?'

By then I knew his voice off by heart.

'As if you didn't know, Sailor.'

'How are you?'

By that time we were enquiring after each other's health, like old mates. Which I suppose we were in a way.

'Can't complain.'

'Good. I wondered if you'd changed your mind.'

'About what?'

'About me. About meeting for a chat.'

I couldn't handle it any more. I knew there was only one way I was going to get rid of him, and that was to do what he wanted.

'All right, Sailor,' I said. 'You win.'

'Do what?'

'You heard.'

'You'll meet me?'

'Do I have any choice?'

'You're a gem, Mr Sharman.'

'It's just for a chat, Sailor. About old times. I'm not promising anything.'

'I know. But I know you'll help me.'

'Don't count on it, son,' I said. 'I'm not in much of a position to help anyone these days. Not even myself.'

'But you were in the papers.'

'That doesn't make me Bob Geldof.'

'Who?'

Sailor had clearly been selective in what he read when he was inside.

'Never mind,' I said. 'Where and when?'

'How about tomorrow midday?'

He obviously believed in striking whilst the iron was hot.

'I'll check my social calendar,' I said. 'No. You're all right. No one's taking me out to lunch at the Caprice. Where-abouts?'

'Well, I'm moving around at the minute. Staying with people. You know how it is.'

Dossing down, he meant.

'I know how it is,' I said. 'But I thought when you were on licence you had to have a fixed address.'

'You are. I gave them me uncle's, but we don't get on. Anyway, I'm in Deptford tonight. D'you know a boozer called the Live And Let Live?'

'No.'

'It's off Creek Road. Going down to the river. Deptford Green, I think it is.'

'Sounds attractive.'

'It'll do,' he said.

'I'll find it,' I said.

'I'll be in there about twelve. Saloon bar. Got a nice view of Greenwich Reach. It reminds me of me days at sea. And I like to see a bit of space these days. It's with being banged up for so long.'

I didn't want to get into his memoirs. And suddenly I didn't want to go at all. My heart sank at the thought of meeting an ex-con in a dump of a boozer, in a scruffy part of town, and listen to him bellyache about ancient history.

Or did I suddenly remember that night in the interview room, and Collier and Lenny Millar beating the shit out of Sailor, and me doing sweet FA about it?

'Look, Sailor,' I said. 'I'll do my best to get there, but I can't promise anything.'

'But you said –'

'I know. But I don't know that it's such a good idea after all.'

'Please.'

How could I resist?

'I'll try,' I said.

'See you then, Mr Sharman, and thanks.'

'Don't thank me yet,' I said, and hung up in his ear.

13

In the end, of course, I went. I knew that I would all along, I suppose. I got up about ten, made myself a bacon sandwich, and drove to Deptford.

I got to the boozer at about twelve. It was close to the old docks. But no one had had the time, energy or money to gentrify that part of south London. It hadn't changed much in twenty-five years, since back in the swinging sixties, when they pulled down the old back-to-backs and stuck up the council tenements, and took all the life out of the place. The Live And Let Live was down at the end of a dusty, dirty, litter-strewn street off Deptford Green. Which was nothing like as colourful as it sounded, and where it looked like the council cleaners hadn't been seen for months. I pushed open the nicotine-coloured door, walked into the saloon bar and looked round for Sailor Grant. I didn't even know if I'd recognise him, but it wasn't hard. He was the only punter in the room. He sat on a red leatherette bench seat, behind a scarred wooden table on which sat a pint of beer, with just a sip taken out of it, a tin of Old Holborn and a packet of green Rizlas. A prison-thin roll-up sat dead in a metal ashtray next to his glass. Next to him was a single, battered khaki bag which probably contained all he owned in the world.

Sailor looked like shit. Worse. His thinness had gone gaunt, until he looked like he was just a step away from a wooden overcoat. His blond hair, what was left of it, was grey, and his face was seamed with more lines than a map of the London underground system.

He looked up as I entered, and his eyes were as dead as the grate of the fireplace in the corner of the bar. I walked over to where he was sitting. 'Mr Sharman,' he said, and his teeth were dark brown in yellow gums. 'I knew you'd come.'

'You knew more than me, then,' I said.

'You're here.'

I felt like asking him: 'What is here?' But I didn't feel like getting into an existential argument right then.

'Yeah,' I said. 'Nice place.'

He looked round the bar. It had seen better days. But then so had he, and for that matter so had I.

'Drink?' I asked.

He half rose to his feet. 'Let me get them in.'

'Save your money,' I said. 'It doesn't look like you made your fortune in jail.'

'I am a bit short.'

'Want a chaser to go with that?' I asked, nodding in the direction of his pint.

'I'll get pissed,' he said. 'I'm not used to strong drink.'

'Didn't you sample the home brew in Wandsworth?' I asked.

'I was on Rule 43, Mr Sharman. You didn't get nothing like that where I was.' Rule 43 is about keeping nonces like Sailor away from the rest for their own safety.

'Well, do you want a short, or not?' I said. 'I haven't got all day.'

'Scotch,' he said.

I went up to the bar, where a barmaid who had also seen better days was cleaning her fingernails with one of the forks that she was wrapping in white paper serviettes.

'Pint of lager and two large Bells,' I said. What the hell? It looked like I was the first person to buy him a drink since we'd nicked him all those years ago. It was the least I could do.

The barmaid got the drinks in the surly way that some staff in the service industries cultivate as a shield against being taken as skivvies. She banged the glasses on to the bar top in front of me, and demanded an extortionately high price in return. I paid without a word and took the drinks back to the table where Sailor was waiting. I could feel her eyes drilling into my back as I walked across the thin, filthy carpet.

It served me right for wanting a drink.

I put the glasses down, pulled over a chair, and sat facing Sailor. He wouldn't look at me. I took a packet of cigarettes out of my pocket and offered him one.

'No, ta,' he said. 'I'm not used to tailor-mades.'

'Was it bad?' I asked, as I lit mine.

'It was hell, Mr Sharman. Honest. You don't know what it's like on the rule landing. Do you know they shit in your food and the screws do nothing about it.'

It's the same all over, I thought. *Everybody's* got to have someone to look down on. Even in prison. Everybody needs a whipping boy to take their spite out on.

'I heard,' I said.

'Shouldn't be allowed,' he said. 'Specially as I never done it.'

'Leave it out, Sailor,' I said. 'It's all ancient history.'

'But *you* know.'

'I don't know anything, Sailor,' I said. 'Sometimes I don't even know who I am.'

'But I want justice.'

I nearly laughed out loud.

Justice. In this world. He had more chance of shitting rubies.

'You're out now,' I said. 'Think yourself lucky you only did a twelve-stretch.'

'They have to let you out quicker these days. Make room for the up-and-comers. There's not enough room inside,' said Sailor.

I shook my head and tasted the beer. It was thin and watery, but at least it was cold. I sipped at the Scotch. It burnt a path down into my stomach where, in a fight to the death, it met the bacon I'd eaten earlier.

'And you reckon I can get you justice, do you?' I asked.

'You could if you wanted.'

'But I don't want, Sailor. I just want to be left alone to get on with my little life. It ain't much, but it's all I've got.'

'I wanted to be left alone to get on with *my* life,' he said, and his voice was loud enough to ruffle the feathers of the barmaid, who switched on the stereo system and chose an Elton John CD to cover the sound of our conversation.

'You and your lot made sure I didn't,' he went on over 'Candle in the Wind'. I hate that fucking song.

'They're not my lot now,' I replied. 'I'm *persona non grata* with them. Have been for years.'

'I know. Word gets round, even when you're on Rule 43. That's just why you could do it.'

I shook my head. 'No chance, Sailor. I prefer to forget that part of my life. Sorry mate.'

'I never done nothing to that girl,' he said, almost sobbing.

I was getting pissed off. Pissed off with the shitty bar I was sitting in. Pissed off with the rubbish beer. Pissed off with the rude barmaid. Pissed off with fucking Elton John singing stupid songs about things he knew nothing about. Pissed off with Sailor and his interminable whining. But mostly pissed off with myself for being who I was.

'But it was only a matter of time, Sailor,' I said. 'Even if you didn't touch Carol Harvey. Eventually you'd have got round to getting bored with showing your dick to little kids. Eventually you'd've wondered what it was like to actually touch them. And then one thing would've led to another, and you'd've ended up just where you did end up. You're a nasty little nonce, Sailor. And I think you probably got exactly what you deserved.' And I left my drinks and got up from the table and took a couple of tenners out of the pocket of my jeans and tossed them down on top of his tobacco tin. 'There's a few quid for you. Don't bother me again.'

And I left and drove back home, pulled the phone plug out of the wall, sat on the sofa and demolished the best part of a bottle of gin before I passed out.

14

After that Sailor didn't ring again. It looked like he'd finally got the message.

For a week or so, things were back to normal.

I was dossing around with Dawn and Tracey most of the time. Business was slack. In fact non-existent. Mainly because I'd turned off the answer machine in my office, and threw the mail into the bin unread on the rare occasions I went down there.

I wasn't going to win any local businessman of the year awards, and that was a fact.

The truth of the matter was I didn't care that much. I was getting on very well without the world, and from what I could see, the world was getting on very well without me.

But, as I might have guessed, if I'd taken time out to think about it, it couldn't last.

Nature abhors a vacuum, and that was exactly what I was living in.

The telephone rang in the middle of the night. I was alone. I tried to ignore it, but it wouldn't go away. I answered it. 'Hello,' I said, as you do.

'Nick Sharman?' said another voice from my past, although once again I didn't recognise it straight off.

'Yes.'

'Hello, Nick. It's Terry Collier.'

'Terry Collier?' I replied with a question mark. Although I remembered him well enough. I'd been thinking about him only a short time before, after all. It was a coincidence that was already worrying me.

'How soon they forget,' he said. 'Come on, son. Wake up. You remember me, don't you?'

'Terry Collier from Brixton nick,' I said. Just for something to say, as I tried to come to.

'Peckham now.'

'What's going on?'

'You're wanted.'

'What for? Overdue parking tickets, or the annual reunion?'

'Don't be smart, son.'

'Is this a joke?' I asked, and even as I said the words, I knew it wasn't.

'Oh no. No joke. As I recall, dead bodies are never a joke.'

I tried to make sense of what he was saying, but my head was still fogged with sleep.

'Say again,' I said.

'We've got a dead body here. A suicide by the looks of it.'

'What's that got to do with me?' But I knew.

'He left a note addressed to you. We thought you might like to come over and read it.'

'Who?' I asked, but I knew that too.

'Your old friend and mine, Sailor Grant.'

'Oh shit.'

'Oh shit, indeed, son. It's not very nice I must say. And we're dying to see you, if you'll excuse the pun.'

'Who's we?'

'Me and Lenny Millar. You remember Lenny. And of course old Sailor. Though I doubt if he'll have much to say to you, being deceased and all. Except for what's in his letter of course.'

'Lenny Millar. Christ, are you two still together?'

'Why split up a winning team. He's a skipper now, and I'm a DI.'

Shit always rises, I thought.

'So come on, Nick. Get your skates on, boy. We haven't got all night.'

But of course, that was precisely what they did have.

'You could just open it without me,' I said.

'We have. And we want you to read it. Now. Here in person.'

'Where is here exactly?'

'The garden of England. Canvey House, Lion Estate, New Cross. Number 22.'

'Not that place.'

'*That* place. So get yourself over here right away. That's official. Understand?'

'Yes,' I said. 'I understand. I'll be with you in a few.' I put down the phone.

I called the local mini-cab office right away, and they promised a car *tout suite*. I knew the Lion Estate of old, and I wasn't taking my car to within a mile of it. I didn't tell the operator exactly where I was going. I just said New Cross.

I rinsed my tired old face and got dressed, and for once the cab was waiting before I'd laced up my boots.

When I told the driver where we were headed, he wasn't happy. He hummed and hawed, and eventually demanded a tenner out front, in case I did a runner. I paid him without argument. Otherwise I knew he'd just turf me out of the car, and that would be that.

I didn't blame him for not wanting to go. If I'd been a cab driver I wouldn't have wanted to take a fare to the Lion Estate either. It was a sink. A black hole where the local council dropped all the tenants it didn't want to know about: the thieves, junkies, arsonists, non-payers of rent, bad neighbours. You name any kind of anti-social behaviour, and there'd be a dozen or so professionals at it on the Lion. It was a no-go area for postmen, milkmen, doctors, dustmen, meter readers, bailiffs, everyone. Social workers were regularly bottled off. The fire service only went in with police protection, and ambulances had stopped entering the estate after three false alarms in as many days ended up with three ambulances being stripped of all drugs, medication and saleable parts. And Canvey House: that was the worst part of a lousy place. It was one of three tower blocks right in the middle of the Lion. The water-stained concrete that it was built of was scarred with smoke, bullet holes, the lot. Inside it was infested with every bug and insect known to man, and probably a few that weren't. It was damp, rotten with mould, and riddled with asbestos. A perpetual hard rain of garbage, old TV sets, furniture and Christ knows what else poured off the building, day and night, because the tenants couldn't be bothered to take their junk downstairs by more conventional means. You took your life in your hands just entering the front door. And once inside, the corridors and lifts were the domain of muggers, dope dealers and sexual perverts.

The cab driver dropped me off at the outskirts of the estate. He point-blank refused to drive into the maze of narrow turnings that covered it. I didn't blame him. Cab hijacking by joy riders was one of the new games on the estate. And his Volvo wasn't in bad nick.

I walked up to Canvey House along pavements covered in Rottweiler shit, tin cans, cardboard pizza-coffins and broken glass, under dead streetlamps that had been vandalised so many times the council didn't even bother to repair them any more. I saw a couple of gangs of youths roaming the place, but both times I stopped in the darkness until they had passed me.

I got to Canvey House at three in the morning. The dark night of the soul. A police Metro was parked next to an unmarked Sierra well away from the building. It's not pleasant to have half a hundredweight of rusty refrigerator drop through the sun roof as you're chatting on the RT.

I went through the gap where the security doors had once stood and into the foyer of the building. If that's not too grand a word for a shit-stinking concrete hall covered in graffiti. I took the stairs. I wasn't about to risk being stuck in the lift with a knife-wielding crackhead or worse. Number 22 was on the sixth floor. The front door was standing ajar, with a uniformed copper outside on guard. I told him who I was, and why I was there, and he called inside for DI Collier. Terry came to the door himself to greet me. It wasn't the friendliest of reunions, but then I hadn't expected it to be.

'Nick Sharman,' he said. 'Well, well, well. It's been a long time. A lot of water under the bridge.'

I nodded. 'Terry,' I said. 'How are you?'

'Save it, son,' he replied. 'We're not here for that. I don't want to see you, any more than you want to see me. I just want you to read what Sailor wrote you. Then we can all fuck off out of this shithole.'

I nodded again. 'Fair enough,' I said.

'Come on in then. The body's still here. The meat wagon's out on another shout. I hope you've got a strong stomach. It's not a pretty sight.'

He looked at the uniform and said, 'You can hop it now, son. We'll take care of the necessary.'

The uniform didn't need to be told twice and made for the stairs without saying a word.

15

I followed Collier into the flat. It stank like a public toilet. The wallpaper in the hall was covered in mould, and there was no carpet on the filthy linoleum floor.

'Come and see your old mate,' he said, and opened the first door on the left.

It was the bathroom. An airless, windowless hutch that stank worse than the hall outside. It wasn't hard to see why.

Next to the filthy bath was the toilet. Sitting on it was Sailor Grant. He was naked. His skinny body was scarred and white. He was slumped back against the cistern and he'd vomited down his bare chest. His arms were hanging down by his sides and his legs were bent at the knees. His face was yellow and in rictus, his lips drawn back over his teeth, and there was so little flesh on his skull it looked like he'd been dead for months. His flaccid cock hung down limply between his legs.

Next to the toilet was a half-bottle of Scotch on its side. There was still a tiny residue of liquor inside it. The outside of the toilet bowl was covered with soft, drying faeces.

'Shit himself,' said Collier, and held up a plastic bag, inside which was a dark brown pill bottle. 'Drunk himself stupid, then took a handful of sleepers. What a way for a bloke like me to spend the night, eh? Stuck in here with that.'

'Goes with the job,' I said. But not necessarily your job, I thought. You'd be too high-powered these days to get involved with a sordid little suicide on the Lion Estate. But I didn't make any comment.

'Course you'd know,' he said sarcastically.

'Who found him?' I asked, ignoring his comment.

'His mate who he squatted this place with. He was sleeping *his* afternoon's recreational drinking off in the back. Woke up, got took short, and found this. Pissed himself, he did. He called us in. He's down the station now making a statement.'

'Where's the letter Sailor left?' I asked.

'In the living room, if you can call it living,' he said. 'Lenny's got it.'

He pushed past me, and I followed him into another room. It didn't smell so bad in there. Just damp and old and loveless. You can smell lovelessness you know. If you're used to it like I was.

Lenny Millar was standing by the window looking down over the lights of the estate. There was nothing to sit on except an orange crate in one corner. The place was as filthy as the rest of the flat I'd seen, and littered with beer cans and more half-bottles of Scotch. All empty this time.

He turned at our entrance. 'Nick Sharman,' he said. 'By Christ, I thought you were dead.'

'No such luck,' said Collier.

Lenny was holding a grubby sheet of paper in his hand. 'This was addressed to you,' he said to me. 'Must've missed the last post. We couldn't resist reading it while we were waiting for you. Hope you don't mind.'

I ignored his comment and, after a second, he handed the letter to me.

I looked at it in the light from the unshaded centre fixture. It was hard to make out the scrawl, but I persevered.

Mr Sharman,
theres nothing here for me on the outside
I thourt you mite be able to help me
You no I never done what they said I done

You were my last chance of cleering my name
I never tuched that girl and we both no thats true.
I dont blame you you were only doing yore job
dont worry ill be better of were im going
best wishes sailor

'Touching, isn't it?' said Collier.

I shrugged, but the note affected me more deeply than he'd ever know. How could anyone write 'best wishes' and then top themselves?

'Were you helping him?' asked Lenny Millar.

'With what?'

'With whatever he was doing. Trying to clear his name, or some such nonsense.'

'No. He asked me, but I blanked him.'

'Sez you.'

'It's the truth.'

'And we're supposed to believe you.'

'I don't often get mixed up in anything these days,' I said. 'That's my life.'

'Your life's shit, Sharman,' said Collier. 'Just shit. I hear you're going case with a pair of bent strippers down Wandsworth way.'

'Why would you hear that?' I asked.

'I like to keep in touch with old colleagues.'

'I just bet you do.'

'Meaning?'

'Meaning nothing. Can I go now? This place is depressing me.'

'Shame. Just make sure you don't get involved, and we'll all be happy.'

'Involved with what? There's nothing *to* get involved in. The poor little fucker done his bird, then got let out to live in a place like this, being hassled by people like you, for something he probably never did in the first place. Like he said in this –' I held up the piece of paper in my hand '– he's probably better off where he is now.'

'And you'd be better off forgetting all about him,' said Collier.

'Who?' I asked, as if I'd already forgotten, and he hesitated. If I hadn't said any more, he'd have probably let me go and get on with whatever I had to get on with. But I never know when to stop. When to leave well enough alone.

'But it's interesting that you're still so worried about him after all this time. Even though he's dead,' I said. 'I wonder why?'

And Collier hit me. A low blow that doubled me over, and introduced me to a world of pain where I was going to live for a long time. I retched, and put out my hand to Lenny for help, but all he did was smile nastily and kick me in the kidneys. I felt more dreadful pain in my back as the blow connected, and Collier moved in and started hitting me again, anywhere he could reach, until the light in the central fixture went out, and I dropped slowly away into a black hole of my own.

16

I came to lying on the cold floor of the flat. I hurt so much that I almost couldn't get a grip on reality. I wavered back into unconsciousness until Lenny Millar threw cold water in my face. I opened my eyes again, snorted as I breathed in the water and looked up into his ugly clock.

'He's come round, guv,' he said. 'What shall I do?'

'Get him up,' said Collier. 'We can't leave him here. That young copper saw him arrive. We'll have to take him away and finish him off somewhere else.'

Charming, I thought. That's me you're talking about.

'Where?' asked Millar.

'The marshes,' said Collier. 'We can lose his body and no one will ever find him.'

This was serious. They were talking calmly about killing me, and I was letting them. I had to try and pull myself together. I licked the water off my lips and swallowed it as if somehow it would help.

'Can't we do for him here?' asked Millar.

'No. See if he can still walk. I don't want to have to carry him out. I want him on two legs however bad he is. Anyone who sees us will think he's pissed or stoned. How unusual round here.'

Millar tugged me to my feet. I held on to him for support as a terrible agony ran down my spine. Fuck me, I reckoned they'd be doing me a favour if they did top me. He shoved me against the wall and snarled up into my face. 'Don't say nothin' to nobody as we go or we'll do for you in front of them. Understand?'

I was silent and he backhanded my face. 'Understand?' he roared.

I managed a nod, but that was about all.

Collier and Millar hustled me out of the flat and down the stairs, my feet dragging as I went. Outside I was hauled over to the Sierra which now stood alone, and Collier opened the driver's door, reached in and released the lock on the passenger door behind it. He yanked it open and Millar shoved me inside, and then joined me on the rear bench seat, slammed the door behind him and savagely slapped down the button that locked it. Collier got behind the wheel and started the engine.

I sat with my head against the lining of the car. I kept floating in and out of consciousness as Collier steered the car through the dark streets of the estate towards the main road. I knew I was a goner unless I did something. But what? I focused my eyes on the lock button of the door on my side. It was less than two feet from my hand and my only chance.

'This is a right fuck-up,' said Millar to the back of Collier's head as we went.

'Will you relax?' said Collier. 'Everything's been all right up to now, hasn't it?'

'Till that git Grant got out of prison and webbed up with this one.' Millar dug me viciously in the ribs and a red mist came down over my eyes.

'It's sorted,' said Collier. 'He'll be out of our hair in an hour.'

'Too many bodies,' said Millar's voice from somewhere on the edge of the galaxy.

'We're minted,' said Collier. 'We've still got that paper.'

'You have, you mean,' said Millar. What the hell were they talking about?

'I earned it,' said Collier. 'If it wasn't for me we wouldn't be sitting here now.'

'Is that supposed to make me feel better?' said Millar. 'A fat lot of

fucking good it'll do us if all this comes out, even after all this time.'
And he was silent.

We turned on to the main drag, which even that late still had
some pedestrian and vehicular traffic. But I knew that the closer
to the marshes we got, the fewer people would be about and that
I would be done for. I concentrated all my attention on the door
button and prayed that the child-proof locks weren't on. If they were
I was fucked. Collier slowed for a red light and I made my move. I
lunged for the lock, flipped it up, hit the door handle and kicked at
the door with all my remaining strength. It opened, and I pushed
back against the seat and threw myself out of the car. I tried to roll
myself into a ball, landed with a jolt on my shoulder, and tumbled
along the blacktop, the impact of my flesh on the tarmac sending
more spasms of pain through my already abused body.

The Sierra skidded to a halt, fifty yards up the road with a scream
of rubber. I turned my head in its direction and saw the reversing
lights come on, and then from between two buildings in front of
me came the most beautiful sight of my life. A uniformed constable
strolled into view. I reached out one hand towards him as, with a
crash of gears, the Sierra leapt forward and took the next sharp corner
on two wheels, and I fell forward on to the kerb and everything went
black again.

17

Things got weird from there on in. I can't remember everything, but what I do remember still comes back from time to time. I don't have a choice of nightmares now. They're always the same.

I woke up in the ambulance, although I didn't know it was an ambulance then. All I could see was a man's face peering down at me. I was wearing an oxygen mask, I suppose. I know that I couldn't speak. But I lifted my hand and saw the streaks of blood that were drying on it.

I woke up again in the hospital. Or maybe I was already dreaming. I was being rushed along a corridor. I tried to speak again, but nothing came out.

Then things got *really* weird.

I was in an operating theatre. Lying there with doctors and nurses clustered round me. I couldn't move or speak. The ECG machine was bleeping quietly away, and everything appeared to be serene. As I looked, I didn't have a worry in the world. Then I heard a voice speak my name, and I looked round. Standing there behind the doctors and nurses was Sailor Grant. He was naked and dead, but it was his voice I heard speak my name, and it seemed like the most natural thing in the world. As I looked into Sailor's face there was a sudden commotion amongst the doctors and nurses standing round me. Everyone in the room was moving fast, and I saw the

ECG machine go flat-line all of a sudden and start to sound a high-pitched scream.

I knew then that it was my choice. If I wanted to live, I could live. If I wanted to die, I could die. I looked up at Sailor again as a doctor laid two paddles on my bare chest, shouted 'clear' and attempted to start my heart.

'You can come with me or stay,' I heard him say. 'But if you stay you must finish what you started all that time ago.'

I knew what he meant. Carol Harvey's murder. I knew that if I decided to live I had to do the right thing by her. I looked up at Sailor's face again as the doctor fibulated me for the second time and I made my decision. Shit, I thought, at least they should let you die in peace.

I woke up under crisp hospital sheets with a pretty nurse smiling down at me. 'We thought we'd lost you,' she said.

My throat was so dry I couldn't speak. She gave me a plastic beaker of water, with a straw sticking out, and I sipped a drop, and it tasted like nectar.

'Bad pennies,' I croaked. 'It's harder to get rid of us than you think.'

'Don't talk,' she told me. 'I'll go and fetch a doctor.'

I lay back on the pillow and admired the design on the plastic curtains that surrounded my bed.

About two minutes later a balding thirty-something in a white coat bustled through a gap in the curtains and stood looking at me.

'So you're back,' he said. 'It's something of a miracle.'

'Is that so?' I asked. 'What happened?'

'There's plenty of time for that,' he said brusquely. 'Let me have a look at you first.'

He gave me an examination, and stood up from the bed shaking his head.

'You shouldn't be here at all,' he said. 'You were clinically dead for a while there.'

'I've got something to do,' I told him. 'Something important.' But he didn't know what the hell I was talking about, and right then neither did I.

He left after that, and the pretty nurse came back. She smelled like clean sheets herself, and I must confess to having carnal thoughts about what she was like under that starched uniform of hers. I had to be getting better.

'How are you feeling?' she asked.

'I don't know,' I said, and begged for more water.

'You've had lots of visitors,' she said. 'Your wife and daughter were here.'

'Ex-wife,' I told her. 'Are they here now?'

She smiled. 'No. That was weeks ago. You've been unconscious for ages.'

I suddenly felt alarmed. 'How long?' I demanded.

She looked at my charts. 'You were brought in here over six weeks ago.'

'Six weeks,' I said. 'Christ, what's the date?'

'September the first.'

Jesus, I thought. That's impossible.

'And your two girlfriends keep coming in to see you.'

'Dawn and Tracey?' I said.

'Yes. They're ever so nice. They said they'd come in and entertain the patients if we wanted.'

'I bet they would,' I said. 'Trouble is they might kill some whilst they're at it.'

'And the police,' she said. 'They want to know what happened.'

'So do I,' I told her. And I did. Because at that precise moment I couldn't remember a damn thing.

So she sat down on the chair beside the bed and told me what she did know.

18

Which wasn't a great amount. I'd been brought into King's College Hospital, after being picked up from the gutter. I'd been badly beaten.

I had a ruptured spleen, a couple of broken ribs, a collapsed lung, a fractured collarbone, extensive bruising. Plus a lot of superficial cuts and mild concussion. I'd been rushed to theatre for an operation on the spleen. There had been complications on the operating table, and my heart had stopped. The doctors had called a crash code, and I'd been brought back to life after dying for half a minute or so.

I'd been out of it for six weeks. Not in a coma as such, but pretty close. I'd mumbled and shouted, and fought the people who were trying to help me, but I hadn't opened my eyes until earlier that day when, alerted by the fact that I was trying to speak again, the nurse had come to my bedside.

Simple.

Except I couldn't remember what had happened.

Not then.

That had been the middle of July. Now it was the first of September.

The last thing I did remember was a Sunday night out with Dawn and Tracey. A simple trip down the pub, followed by a Chinese meal, and a fuck with Dawn. But I knew that had been in June. Just after my birthday. After that nothing.

Not then.

'Well, nurse,' I said. 'Another fine mess I seem to have got myself into.'

'Do you want a mirror?' she asked.

'Why?' I said. 'Did you have to do plastic surgery?'

'No. I thought you just might like to see.'

'OK,' I said. 'You're the boss.'

She gave me a mirror from inside the drawer of the cupboard next to my bed. I looked at myself. My face was thinner. My hair was longer, but apart from that I was pretty much as I remembered. Not that I'd exactly call that pretty. 'Yeah,' I said. 'That's me all right. Who's been shaving me?'

'I have,' she said.

'Thanks.'

'It's been a pleasure. Do you want me to tell anyone you're back in the land of the living?'

'Not the taxman,' I said.

She giggled. 'You're funny,' she said.

I looked at the swell of her breasts under the starched uniform and wondered again what she looked like without it.

'You could tell Dawn and Tracey.'

'I'll call them for you. They left a number with sister.'

'You're very kind. What's your name by the way?'

'Pru.'

'That's nice.'

'So I've been told. I'll go and make that call.' And she left.

She wasn't gone for long, and when she did come back, she didn't bring good news. 'You've got a visitor,' she said.

'Who?'

'A policeman. There've been lots.'

'I just bet there have.'

'This one's been before. He's horrible.' She shuddered.

'What's his name?' I asked.

Suddenly the curtains round the bed were pushed aside, and an unkempt figure in a greasy old raincoat stuck his head and shoulders inside. He smiled when he saw me.

'Inspector Robber,' I said.

'Who were you expecting?'

'Columbo. But I see you got your dibs on the mac today.'

'Amusing, Sharman. I see they didn't knock your sense of humour out of you. I'm glad about that.'

'Who didn't?' I asked.

'Whoever knocked the other seven kinds of shit out of you. Beg your pardon, miss.' And he gave Pru a cheesy smile that showed where he'd missed with the toothbrush that morning.

'That's all right,' she said sniffily. 'I've heard worse. But I thought I told you to wait outside until I found out whether Mr Sharman wanted to see you or not.'

'As if he wouldn't,' said Robber.

'As if,' I said. 'It's OK, Pru. Let him stay.'

'If you're sure.'

I nodded, and she left with a swish of starched skirts.

'Pru, is it?' said Robber. 'You don't waste much time.'

'Charmers like us don't have to. You must have noticed that yourself.'

Robber didn't reply, just drew up a chair and sat down. It gave me a chance to give him the once over.

He hadn't changed. He still looked exactly like the last time I'd seen him, when I'd got involved in a case he'd been working on. It had finished in tears, but then most of my cases did. He still didn't know the whole story, and he never would.

His hair was greasy. His skin was greasy. His mac was greasy. His shirt was a disgrace, and his neck bulged over the dirty, too-tight collar fastened with a safety pin under the knot of his greasy old tie. His trousers had never met an iron, and his shoes were ill-acquainted with polish. In short, he was a mess. I could never work out what he did with all the money he earned.

'So what's the story?' he asked when he was comfortable and had a cigarette lit.

'No smoking in here,' I said.

He shrugged.

'Give us a drag then.'

He did. The end was wet, but the smoke tasted good.

'Who did it, Sharman?' he asked.

'Good question. I don't remember.'

'Excuse no. 65A. I don't remember, your honour. Me mind's a complete blank.'

'Your honour, bollocks. I'm not on trial, am I?'

He shrugged again.

'Well, am I?'

'Not at the moment.'

'Listen,' I said. 'As far as I understand, it was me that took a beating. Maybe if you found out who did it, *they* might be on trial.'

'Who, is difficult,' he said. 'Why, might help.'

'Jack,' I said, taking the liberty of using his Christian name. 'If I knew, I'd tell you. Honest. But the last thing I remember is going out with two young ladies some time in June. After that I'm a blank.'

'Don't tempt me,' he said, and dogged his ciggie out in a bedpan. 'If you do remember anything get in touch.'

'Is this official?' I asked.

'Half and half. I'm interested.'

'I'm flattered.'

'So you should be.' He stood up to leave.

'Is that it?' I asked.

'For now. I shall return.'

'Like General MacArthur.'

The remark went right over his head.

'No "I'm glad you're better"?' I asked.

'Don't fuck about, Sharman. You know the world would be a better place without you.' He pushed out through the curtains again.

My, but that stung.

19

That night they must have cut my medication. Or maybe it was because it was my first night back in the world. Or something. Who knows?

But whatever it was, it was the first night that I had the dreams. The nightmares that still come back regularly to haunt my sleep.

They turned off the main lights in the small ward at about ten. I lay and looked into the shadows until I fell asleep. Then I dreamt about what happened all those weeks ago. Starting at the end and working backwards.

First I was in the operating theatre with the paddles on my chest, and my body jumping as the electrical current went through it. I saw Sailor Grant's dead body and I remembered his words, and decided that, however shitty it was, living was preferable to dying. Then I was in the hospital corridor being rushed to the theatre, then the ambulance.

Then I started to remember the really bad bits.

It was like the memory of an acid trip. Or a film that had been burnt and melted.

I dreamed about being driven along almost deserted streets, and a conversation about a piece of paper, that somehow was important, but I didn't know why. And leaping from the car to bounce across the tarmac until I ended up in the gutter and saw that copper. The man who saved my life. After that I dreamed I was being beaten.

Beaten hard by experts. Collier and Millar. Punching, kicking and gouging, until they nearly killed me. And then hearing that was what they intended to do.

I dreamed of Sailor's dead body on the toilet, and then that memory got mixed up with the Sailor Grant I saw in the operating theatre, and in the Live And Let Live. All asking for my help. And all being turned down.

I came awake in the middle of the night, struggling to sit up, a silent scream bubbling in the back of my throat.

Then I remembered.

I remembered everything, and resolved to do something about it.

I had to stay at King's for another three weeks, convalescing.

I had lots more visitors.

My mother roused herself from deepest Sussex to make the pilgrimage to the big, wicked city, and brought me some sandwiches. Thanks, Mum. She didn't stay long. Just as well probably.

My ex-wife and daughter came down again from Aberdeen. Judith had grown up since the last time I'd seen her. A real young lady, dressed in the latest rave fashions. It made me feel quite old to look at her. Laura was ageing well. Maybe it was the Scottish air. They looked more like two sisters than mother and daughter. Mind you, her disposition hadn't improved much. She moaned and groaned so much about the cost of the air fares down to London that I offered her a cheque to pay for them.

Christ. We were married once. Love, honour and fucking obey. Bitch.

At least she had the good grace to refuse the money. And why shouldn't she? Her husband was rolling in it. But, if Judith hadn't been there, I think she might just have taken it, out of spite.

Dawn and Tracey were in and out all the time. What a popular pair they were with the other male patients, and doctors in particular.

They actually rolled in when Laura and Judith were there one afternoon. The girls were on their way to a masonic do in Clerkenwell, where they were going to take off every stitch in honour of the Great Architect.

Laura's face was a picture. There they came, the Wandsworth two. Staggering in on the latest glam-rock revival: platform sole and pencil heel, toeless, suede St Louis Blues, their passage not helped by the two or three Drambuie-and-lagers they'd sucked down for lunch. With the shoes, Tracey had opted for a long, tight skirt that was split to the thigh, black fishnet tights, a patchwork tank top sans bra, and a red satin jacket with Concorde lapels. When Tracey went for a look she really went for it. And since I'd been in hospital the '70s had obviously returned with a vengeance.

Dawn had stuck with the basic Soho streetwalker image that she loved. Black stockings, with a thin gold chain around the right ankle, black mini-skirt that just covered the tops of them, black satin blouse, unbuttoned to show the lace of her black net bra, and the black shiny plastic mac that the girls took turns to wear. On top of her blonde head, at a rakish angle, was set a black beret. Her slap consisted of solid-state pan stick, sooty mascara, and shiny red Monroe lipstick. Tracey had gone for a full rainbow psychedelic '70s make-up job to go with the rest of her outfit.

Those two would stop traffic on Resurrection Day. And probably will.

As they pushed their way through the ward door and wobbled over to my bed, Laura turned and said, 'I imagine these two are with you.'

I just nodded.

Judith was gobsmacked by the sight of them.

'Hello, Nick,' said Tracey. 'Fuck me, have we had a journey today. Old Bill gave us a pull in Herne Hill. I think they thought we was on the game or sumfin'.' She suddenly noticed Judith and Laura. 'Sorry,' she said. 'Are we interruptin' anyfin'?' When Tracey was agitated, her accent zeroed in on Bermondsey where she'd been born and bred, and nothing would get it any further up river.

Except a stiff drink that is.

'No,' I said mildly. 'Not a thing. This is my ex-wife Laura, and this is my –' I almost said 'little girl', before I realised, just in time, the kind of look that Judith would give me if I did '– daughter, Judith. This is Dawn and Tracey. Friends of mine. They've been visiting almost every day to make sure I'm all right.'

Laura managed a smile that would curdle milk, and offered her hand like the Queen Mother unveiling a war memorial. Judith swallowed and said, 'Hi.'

'I like your 'at,' said Tracey, referring to Judith's backwards-facing baseball cap. 'Dead good, eh, Dawn?'

'Wicked,' Dawn replied. 'Mind if I sit down, Nick? These bleeding shoes might look the business, but they're murder on my poor old feet.'

She collapsed on to the edge of the bed, and her skirt shot up over the tops of her stockings to expose three inches of milk-white thighs, bisected by black suspenders. Poor Laura almost fainted dead away.

She used to be as horny as fuck herself once. And nothing fazed her. I always find it sad when people change.

Tracey sat on the other side of the bed and looked long and hard at me.

I hadn't told anyone what had happened that night on the Lion, and how I ended up in a gutter in Peckham. If anyone asked, and they did, including two local CID who I'd never met before, and didn't particularly want to meet again, I told them I couldn't remember. That I must have been mugged. The fact that I'd still had my wallet on me when I was picked up, cash and ID intact, sort of blew that one out of the water, but there you go.

'You look much better, Nick,' Tracey said.

'Good,' I said. 'I'm glad you think so. I feel much better, too.'

'We'll have you right as rain in no time, as soon as you're out of this dump. Eh, Dawn?'

'Course we will,' Dawn replied. 'Some good home cooking and you'll be tickety-boo.'

I felt like I was beginning to hallucinate again. Tracey and Dawn's idea of home cooking was ten minutes in the microwave at full blast for anything from a TV dinner to a five-pound oven-ready chicken. I expect the domestic bit was for Laura's benefit.

'I can't wait,' I said.

'You from round 'ere?' Tracey asked Laura.

'Aberdeen actually,' replied Laura in her best lady-of-the-manor fashion. She was beginning to piss me right off. Tracey and Dawn were genuine twenty-four carat. And they gave a shit about me. Which was more than my ex-wife had done for more years than I cared to remember. And she was treating them like they were dirt. Or perhaps I was being too hard on her. At least she'd come down. And brought Judith. She needn't have bothered. Or perhaps it was that I'd never got over the fact that she'd dumped me, even though I'd asked for it. Who can tell with human nature?

'Where you staying?' asked Tracey.

'The Connaught,' replied Laura. 'We always stay there when we're in town.'

And she was moaning about money.

I saw the look that Tracey gave Dawn. I just knew that the guns were coming out. With a vengeance.

'We done a show there once, remember, Dawn?' she said.

I winced. I knew we were in for some memoirs from the skin game, probably in extremely graphic detail, and I just knew that Laura would have a fit.

'Are you singers?' asked Judith, who suddenly found her voice and saved the day.

'No, love,' said Dawn. 'We're…' And she suddenly fell in with how old Judith was. '… Well sort of. All-round entertainers, really.' And she winked at Trace, who, thank God, fell in too, bless her.

'That's right, Judith love,' she said. 'All-round entertainers. That's us.'

Laura obviously wasn't so sure. 'We'd better be going and leave you with your friends, Nick,' she said. 'We'll pop in later. You know we're off first thing tomorrow.'

'OK, Laura,' I said, and winked at Judith. 'Going shopping?' I asked.

Judith nodded.

'Spend lots of Louis's money,' I said. 'I'm sure he won't mind.'

Laura scowled, gathered her things together, and she and Judith left.

'Who's Louis?' asked Dawn

'Her husband.'

'Were you really married to her?' asked Tracey. 'She looks like she's got sandpaper in her knickers.'

I had to laugh. What a woman.

'But your daughter seems nice,' she went on.

'She gets that from me,' I said.

'God help her then,' said Dawn.

I had lots of other visitors too. Des, my old mate from Covent Garden, came in to see me. And my two friends who had been christened Charles: Charlie, the mechanic who serviced my cars; and Chas who worked on the *South London Press*, and who'd got involved with me on a recent case.

Charlie didn't ask what had happened to me. He wasn't the inquisitive type, except when it came to working out why a car wouldn't start.

Chas, on the other hand, was full of questions. Like the rest, I told him I couldn't remember.

He believed me like he believed that the Pope was a Jew.

Robber came back a couple times too. Nosing about to see what he could find. But I just took the piss until he went away again.

Other people came too. Too numerous to mention really. Some I expected, and some I was surprised to see.

But the biggest surprise of all was the day before I was due to be discharged, when Detective Inspector Terry Collier paid me a visit.

I don't mind telling you that the sight of him scared me half to death, if you'll excuse the expression.

I was still dreaming about what happened that night on the Lion – not pleasant dreams as you can imagine – and when he walked into the ward for real my mouth went dry and I felt the sweat break out all over my body. Pure fear. And he knew it.

And I knew that until he was out of circulation one way or another, the mere thought of him would always have that effect on me.

He strolled up to the side of my bed and said, 'Hello, Nick. How's your bad luck?'

'All the worse for seeing you,' I replied.

I didn't want him to know just how scared I *was*.

'That's not a nice thing to say when an old friend and colleague comes calling. I'd've bought you flowers, but the shop was shut.'

'Thanks for the thought,' I said. 'But you needn't have bothered.'

'No bother. I just thought I'd pop in to see how you were getting on. I hear you're off home tomorrow.'

'That's right.'

'Had any other visitors from the force?'

'As if you didn't know.'

He pretended to look hurt. 'Well, have you?'

'Sure I have. A couple of local DCs, and an old friend of mine too.'

'Who?'

'Jack Robber.'

'What did he want?'

'To find out who put me here.'

'But you didn't tell.'

I shook my head.

'So what *did* you tell them?'

'Nothing. That I didn't know what did happen. And you know that too, Collier. Otherwise they'd have been round to see you and your mate.'

'Just checking.'

'You've got some fucking nerve coming here,' I said. And I could feel the sweat break out on my upper lip.

'Is that right?'

'You were going to kill me that night.'

'Fuck off. Course not.'

'I remember.'

'No mate. You were too badly off.' He sat on the edge of the bed, just like an old friend come to call.

'I suppose I took a nasty fall. Like Grant did in the station that night.'

'No mate. You took what you deserved. We'd been waiting a long time for that. And forget all about Grant. He was just a nasty little nonce. You're the last person I would have expected to stick up for one of them. You saw enough of that in the job, didn't you?'

I didn't reply. I was at a disadvantage, being still weak and all tucked up in bed, and he knew it.

'So do yourself a favour,' he went on. 'Keep your nose out of what doesn't concern you any more. We know who your friends are, and where they are, and what they do. It would be a terrible shame if something bad happened to one of them.'

I came off the bed, fists clenched. 'You bastard. Leave my friends out of this,' I shouted, and I saw heads turn right along the ward.

'Keep your voice down,' said Collier. 'We don't want everyone listening in on our business. Now look here, Sharman. You had a result that night. Don't push your luck. Next time you might not.'

Jesus. Next time. That's what I was frightened of.

'Forget about Grant, and forget everything else that happened. Like I said, next time you might not be so lucky. And those tarts of yours who keep coming in to look after you. They might not be so lucky either. You've had a couple of months in here at the taxpayers' expense. How bad? Just go home and get well, and look after your own backyard in future. Understand?'

I understood only too well. The thought of him and Millar getting hold of Tracey and Dawn made me go cold all over.

'You as much as touch those two, and –'

'Don't be silly,' he said. 'Don't act tough with me. You've been nearly shitting your pants since I came in. I asked you if you understood.'

I nodded. What was the point of pretending. He had me exactly where he wanted me.

'Good,' he said. 'So we both understand each other. I like that. Well, I'll be off now. People to see, places to go. You know how it is. With any luck we'll never see each other again. Goodbye, Sharman.' He stuck out his hand for me to shake.

Christ, but that was about the last straw.

I ignored it. Brave boy, aren't I?

'Please yourself,' he said, and turned on his heel and left.

But I'm not dead yet, I thought, as he swaggered out of the ward. And it'll be a long time before you and your mate get another go. And it can't be just a miscarriage of justice twelve years ago that you're so worried about. There's something more. A lot more. And it all has to do with a piece of paper that you have. A piece of paper that, thank God, I didn't mention, and you've probably forgotten I even know about.

You made a mistake, Collier. A mistake that one day you're going to pay for.

You didn't kill me when you had the chance.

20

Dawn and Tracey took me home in their little Renault Five. They'd been round to the flat and given it a good going-over, and filled the fridge up with goodies from the Marks and Sparks chilled cabinets.

I was still a bit weak and wobbly, but I'd get better. I had to. There was a lot to do.

I started off by explaining to them exactly what had happened the night I was beaten almost to death, and the events that had led up to it.

I thought it was the right thing to do. No, I *knew* it was the right thing to do. Terry Collier had threatened them as well as me. If they wanted to split, now was the time.

When I'd finished the story and a bottle of weak French lager, I said, 'I don't want to put you two into any danger. These people are bad. And they're powerful. We aren't. There's lots of ways they can get to us. There's only one way to get to them. I have to find out what really happened that day in Brixton. For some reason Collier and Grisham and Millar needed a scapegoat. They had Sailor, and they done him up like a kipper. I don't know why, but I intend to find out. It's obvious that I was right all along. He didn't rape and kill that girl, but for sure someone did. I'm not going to be safe from those bastards until I find out who. And if you stick around, nor will you be. Maybe I should have told you before. Maybe not. I don't know. Maybe I was just being selfish about it. You were great to me in hospital. And coming round here, doing the cleaning, doing the shopping, I appreciate it. But now might be the time for you to leave. Collier's been keeping an eye on all of us since Sailor came out of prison. He knew about us being together, and it's damn sure he'll know if you don't see me any more. Maybe you'll be safe then. I mean the bloke's crazy. Maybe it won't make any difference. Maybe he intends to hurt anyone I'm fond of just out of spite. I know he's capable of it. That's the trouble. I don't know what he intends to do. I don't know exactly how crazy he is. But I *do* know that he and Millar were going to kill me that night, and I was lucky to get out of that car when I did.

'And if he does hurt you, I'll never forgive myself. It's bad enough that Sailor topped himself. If I'd listened when he came out of jail, perhaps he wouldn't have. If I'd've listened all those years ago in Brixton nick, it's for sure he wouldn't have. I've got to live with that. What I couldn't live with is if either of you got hurt. So I think that it would be better all round if you just left now, and forgot that I ever existed.'

Dawn, who was sitting on the sofa next to Tracey, went and got me another beer. I was in bed. Like I said, I was still a bit weak.

When she returned and sat next to me on the edge of the bed she said, 'You're sure they were going to kill you?'

'Damn sure. They were going to take me up the marshes and bury me.'

'Dirty sluices,' exploded Tracey. 'If I ever get my hands on them –'

'Don't even think about it,' I interrupted.

'Who do you think did kill that girl – Carol Harvey, was it?' said Dawn.

'I don't know, but I think that Collier and Millar do, and maybe Grisham too, the other officer involved. It was for sure that something weird went down the night they beat the confession out of Grant.'

'But they never told you.'

'I'd only just arrived on the strength. They didn't know if they could trust me.'

'So what are you going to do?' Dawn asked.

'Get a portfolio together. Find out where all the main characters are now, and what they're doing. Write out the story, or at least the parts I know of it, and try and make some sense of it. There's so few people I can speak to, see. I don't really know, Dawn, to tell you the truth. But I'm supposed to be a detective. Maybe I can detect what really happened. Find out what this piece of paper is. If it's anything at all, and not just a figment of my imagination. I was pretty bad when I heard them talking. Maybe I heard them wrong.'

'Can we help?'

'Sure. Course you can. I'm not going to be too mobile for a bit. But if you do, we've got to be careful. If Collier and his mob find out what I'm up to, the shit will really hit the fan. And I don't mean maybe.'

Dawn looked at Tracey. 'What do you reckon, Trace?'

Tracey shrugged. 'I couldn't care less,' she said. 'It might be a bit of a laugh.'

'It might not and all,' I interrupted. 'It's serious this. Deadly serious. You two are vulnerable, what with the way you earn. They could bust you in a minute.'

'Fuck 'em,' said Dawn. 'I think you're getting us confused with people who give a shit.'

It was exactly what I'd wanted her to say.

21

So that was that. Enough said, and we didn't mention it again that night.

'Want a joint?' asked Dawn.

'I don't mind,' I said.

'Want another beer?' asked Tracey.

I nodded. 'Are you two working tonight?'

Dawn shook her head as she took a ready-rolled joint out of her handbag. 'No. Tracey's got a date. I thought I'd stay and keep you company. Is that all right?'

'Course it is.'

Tracey went to the kitchen for my beer, came back, and when she handed it to me, kissed me on the cheek. 'I'd better be off,' she said. 'Can't keep my gentleman waiting. Now you two be good and don't do anything I wouldn't.' And she collected her jacket and left.

'Do you want something to eat?' asked Dawn.

'I'm OK. Maybe later.'

'There's plenty in.'

'Good home cooking, eh?'

She smiled. 'As good as Marks can do.'

She lit the joint, took a hit and passed it to me. I popped the tab on the can that Tracey had given me. It was freezing cold, and I had to catch the froth quickly in my mouth.

She was a lot smarter than she let on, was Dawn. A couple of times she'd started to talk to me about her life, and it wasn't like her talking at all. Not like the scrubber she pretended to be, and let the world see. Each time she'd done it, she seemed to realise what she was saying and stopped. As if she was embarrassed.

That night she didn't stop.

'You're all right, Nick, do you know that?' she said.

'Am I?'

'Yeah. You're like us. Bent.'

'Am I?' I asked again. 'You reckon?'

'Not like that, stupid,' she said. 'Not gay. *Bent*. Not straight. Know what I mean?'

'Yes.'

'You couldn't be straight if you tried. I bet deep down inside you always knew that, didn't you?'

I shrugged. She wanted to talk, so I just let her.

'But you did try. You must have. How could you have been a copper, and married an uptight cow like that Laura, or whatever her name was, otherwise?'

She knew exactly what her name was.

'Mind, your daughter was sweet. She *is* like you. I could tell. Poor baby. You just hope she doesn't end up like you. No, you couldn't be straight. You're like us. Me and Trace. You don't give a fuck. Not on the outside anyway. Nobody knows what goes on inside though, do they, Nick?'

I shook my head.

'Did she leave you?' she asked.

'Who?'

'Your wife.'

I nodded.

'Why?' She shook her blonde mop. 'Sorry, I shouldn't ask things like that. You don't have to tell me if you don't want to.'

'It doesn't matter,' I said. 'It's history now. Ancient history.'

Dawn didn't say anything, and I knew she wanted me to tell her.

'It's the old, old story, darlin',' I said. 'I was screwing other women. Lots of other women. Taking a shitload of drugs. I was never at home. You know the sort of thing. But worst of all I didn't love her enough.'

'No man *ever* loves a woman enough,' Dawn said.

'That's a pretty profound statement.'

'True though.'

'You might be right. I'm the wrong person to ask. Laura said I had an emotional death wish.'

'And did you? Do you?'

'Maybe I did. I can't remember. Maybe I still do. I don't know.'

'No wonder you're so fucked up,' she said.

'Who, me?'

'Yes, you. Totally screwed.'

I shrugged. 'Maybe I am, babe,' I said. 'But what can I do about it? It's what I am. What you see is what you get, and that's a fact.'

I lit a cigarette and leaned back on the pillow and drank some more beer.

'And that's the thing I like most about you,' said Dawn. 'See. Most people think what me and Trace do is sick. Loving each other. How can love be sick? But you don't care. I've seen you looking at the people you've met with us: TVs, TSs, other dykes, gay blokes, the Skin Two mob. A lot of people get upset by them. You, you just carry on like it's perfectly natural. You couldn't give a fuck.'

'Why should I?' I said. 'They don't interfere with me. I don't interfere with them. Whatever turns you on. Ain't that right?'

'Sure. But not everybody sees it like that. Do you know what I think, Nick?'

'What?' I said.

'I don't think you're really alive until you've died a bit. And the first time I ever saw you, in that club that afternoon, sitting all alone, not saying nothing, just watching and listening, I knew that you'd died a bit. You have, haven't you?'

I nodded again.

'Some people don't,' she went on. 'Nothing ever happens to them. They live all their lives without anything really bad happening. Then they die. But I don't call that living at all. Then there's others. The ones I feel really sorry for. They do everything right all their lives.

Work, get married, have kids, get a mortgage. And then suddenly one day they die a bit. You see them on TV. On the news. Their kid's been snatched, or someone close has been murdered. You can see it in their faces. They're going bent on nationwide TV. And you just know they're never going to be able to handle it.

'But people like us, we're different. We *can* handle it. It's like we belong to a club. We've always been different. Always been bent. We're survivors. Like we've had thousands of little cuts all our lives, until one cut goes so deep and hurts so much that no one is ever going to be able to cut you that deep again. The scar's so hard that nothing can get through.'

In a way she was right.

'What was yours?' I asked.

'My husband and my baby… You never knew I was married, did you, Nick?'

I shook my head.

'I was only a kid. Seventeen. Still at school. And I was clever too. I was taking A levels, and I could have gone to university. But I had to have a boyfriend. I had to know what it was all about. Be grown up. And then I fell for the baby. So we got married. I couldn't have had an abortion. I would never have forgiven myself. My baby was born on my eighteenth birthday. She'd be twelve now. That's about the same age as your daughter, isn't it?'

I nodded for a third time.

'Kim, we called her. That was his idea. And he really loved her. He wasn't really all that bright. But that didn't matter. He'd've done anything for that baby. And for me. But differently, if you know what I mean. He worshipped Kim from the day she was born. He was a real dad. And he wasn't much more than a kid himself. He changed her nappies. Bathed her. Fed her. Took her out in the pram. He loved it. And he was such a man. I really loved him too. I'd never as much as looked at another bloke since the day I met him.

'He was in the building game. And did he work. He'd do anything. And we were happy then. I'll never forget that. Being happy. It's been such a long time since I was. Really happy, I mean.

'Yeah, we were content, Nick. We had each other, and Kim, and a little money coming in regularly. And the old house at the back of East Street that we'd bought cheap, and he did up till it was like a palace.

'He started out on his own after a bit. Bought a van. Then one Friday it happened. I was working part time in the launderette down the road from where we lived, and he had a big job on, and his mum said she'd take Kim. His mum and dad had moved down towards Kent by then, and we were still in Walworth. But what with the motorway being built, it hardly took any time to get down there. So he set off really early to drop Kim off. He'd fitted one of those baby seats for her in the van. A real good job he did too. It was anchored to the floor of the van with great big bolts. Afterwards the police said it was the only part of the van that was still where it started out.'

She was crying by then, but I didn't comfort her. She didn't want comfort, I could tell. Just to remember and to talk about it to someone. So I let her get on with it.

'They said he was going down the motorway at about fifty in the slow lane. They had witnesses. But even if they hadn't, I know he'd never go fast, not with Kim on board. Then all of a sudden one of those banks of fog you read about came down, out of nowhere. One minute the sun was shining and you could see for miles. The next you couldn't see the end of the bonnet. People were driving into that fog at a hundred miles an hour or more.'

She shook her head at the futility of it.

'A thirty-ton truck hit him up the backside. Pushed him into another truck that had stopped dead in the fog. Him and Kim were both killed outright. Crushed. They wouldn't let me see the bodies, said it would be too much. I wanted to, but they wouldn't let me.

'It wouldn't have mattered though. How bad they were. Because the day they died, I died. I was just twenty when it happened. And they were all there to help me. His mates. They were queuing up to help me. Help themselves more like. And do you know I was in bed with one of them the night after they were both killed? I was so alone and lonely that I let one of them have me. He brought round a bottle of Scotch and a load of grass. I'd never smoked a joint before that night, believe it or not. It made me so horny it hurt. My little family hadn't been dead for two days and I was fucking my husband's best mate. Lovely, eh?'

She was crying harder, and her eyes were bruised from rubbing the tears away. But still I left her alone.

'I ended up in bed with most of them in the end,' she went on. 'It was just for a bit of comfort really. A bit of company at night. But with that lot, you couldn't have company without the other. Know what I mean? But none of them were like him. Not even close. He was a real athlete. In bed and out of it. He was a lovely boy. Some of his mates got a bit heavy too. See, they thought I was weak and vulnerable. A soft touch. But I wasn't. By then the scar was too deep. I went case with them because I wanted to. They didn't like it being my choice and not theirs. And what was worse was that, after a bit, they knew they couldn't hurt me. Not inside. Not where it matters. I didn't give a shit for any of them really. I didn't care if they went back with their wives or out with some other sort. I didn't give a monkey's. So I s'pose they thought that if they couldn't hurt me emotionally, they could hurt me physically.

'One in particular. I made the mistake of moving in with him. I'd sold the house long ago, and pissed most of the money away. I didn't care, see. I was dead, so what did it matter? Anyway, I moved in with this bloke. Eddie Spinetti his name was. I called him Eddie Spaghetti. He didn't like that. But I didn't care. He used to beat the shit out of me. He was a bad bastard, Nick, and I took it for nearly a year. Then I went to a woman's shelter in Balham. I couldn't handle it any more. Just left all my stuff and fucked off. That was where I met Liz. She used to help out at the place. A real bull dyke. At first she scared me more than Eddie did. But she was kind. She sort of took me under her wing. I told her all about Eddie. Then he found out where I was, and came round one afternoon. He busted the front door of the place down and came looking for me in my room. That was in the old days when the pubs used to shut at three. Remember?'

How could I forget?

'I remember,' I said.

'Liz had been out for a drink with a couple of her mates. All three of them bulls, and built like brick shithouses. They arrived at the shelter just as Eddie was kicking down my room door. They picked him up and took him out the back and gave him some of his own medicine. Then they dumped him outside Balham tube. Christ, they didn't mess around. He ended up worse than you did. He lost a kidney. In hospital for four months, he was. And they went in and visited him. Told him that if he ever bothered me again they'd repeat the performance. And go round his local boozer and tell all his mates that it was women put him in hospital. He couldn't have handled that. He'd been telling everyone he was set on by a gang of skinheads. So I never saw him again. After that I ended up as Liz's *femme*. It was all right too. She didn't have a cock, see. Nothing to prove. And do you know what? I never missed it at all. And she didn't have to beat me up to show me that she loved me.'

'What happened to her?' I asked.

'She was doing a bit of dealing – no, a lot. Old Bill was on her tail. She fucked off to Amsterdam to live. She wanted me to go with her, but I couldn't. My baby and my husband are buried here. I couldn't leave them; I have to walk on the same ground they're part of. Otherwise I don't know what I'd do. Then I met Trace. And I fell for her. Who wouldn't? The soft cow. She's the same as us.'

'Why?'

'She was abused as a kid by her dad. She's mostly over it now. But she still don't trust men.'

'Who can blame her?' I asked.

'You're right. But we trust you, love. I've talked to her about it. We could get it together, you and me. You're the first man I've fucked because I want to, since Eddie. The others have been strictly business. I'd like another baby, see. Another chance. I think you only get one go at life. One turn. And then it's over. And so far, my go's been pretty well messed up. Mind you, I wouldn't leave Trace. I still love her. I can't change that. But we could all live together. Or close. I'd never do nothing with her unless you were there. And I wouldn't mind you screwing her if you both wanted it. As long as I was there too. I wouldn't want you two going off together, though.'

'You're as good as gold, Dawn,' I said. 'Better than gold in fact.'

'I wonder how many birds you've said that to, Nick. Lots, I'll bet.

But they ain't here are they? And I am. So what happened to you, Nick? What killed you inside, before your time?'

I thought about it for a minute before I answered. How everything and everybody I'd ever cared about I'd walked away from, or had been violently snatched out of my grasp.

'You know about my wife divorcing me, and taking Judith away,' I said.

Dawn nodded.

'And some people died,' I said. 'Women. Two were killed. One died of cancer.'

'Girlfriends?' she asked.

'Two were. One was a friend. Two were my fault. One wasn't.'

'And you still feel guilty?'

I nodded.

'I thought it was something like that,' said Dawn. 'Do you want to tell me about them?'

I shook my head. 'Not now,' I said. 'Maybe another time.'

'That's all right. One lot of true confessions is probably enough for one night. So what about it? Do you think we could get it together?'

I shrugged again. 'I don't know, babe,' I said. 'It's never occurred to me. I didn't know that was what you wanted.'

'I don't know that I do,' she replied. 'But it might work. You never know.'

'No you don't,' I said.

'Think about it,' she said, and winked, and got up and started to undress. 'I'll just pop into bed with you and show you what you'd be missing if you say no.'

And she did.

22

The next morning we started to gather the evidence together. Dawn bought me a cardboard-covered exercise book to write in. On the front was a drawing of a galleon under full sail. I liked that. It seemed like a very apt illustration for a book about a sailor.

I started off by writing down everything I remembered about the case. From day one. At the same time, quietly, we began to gather information. It's not difficult if you've got the front and know what to say. The girls were great. Theatrical training, see.

We started off with the police officers involved.

All but one had done fairly well over the past dozen or so years.

Superintendent Byrne had done the best. He'd risen to become Assistant Commissioner of the Metropolitan Police, a very senior post. He'd retired three years previously to live with his wife in a large detached house in its own grounds in Redhill. He'd received the MBE on his retirement, and there was talk of a knighthood within a few years.

DI Grisham was now a commander in the flying squad, the legendary Sweeney. He was based at New Scotland Yard, and was a big man in the Job. He lived alone in a detached house in Dulwich.

Sergeant Terry Collier was, as I knew to my own cost, now a DI at Peckham, on the same squad as Millar who had stalled at the rank of Detective Sergeant. Collier was divorced, and had a tiny house in a new development on the Peckham ground. Millar had a semi outside Croydon where he lived with his wife and two kids.

DI Harvey was the only loser.

He'd had a rough time of it all those years ago. Firstly his wife had died four years before Carol had been killed. Apparently he'd done a good job of bringing up his two daughters on his own. He'd been promoted to Detective Inspector two years before the murder took place, but then it had all started to fall apart for him.

Harvey had taken to the booze in a big way after the crime had been committed. And his work had suffered. Eventually he'd taken a demotion to uniformed sergeant, and been transferred to the traffic section at Lewes. He was still there to this day, apparently a demoralized and bitter man.

Who the hell could blame him?

I borrowed a car off Charlie. An old Vauxhall Cavalier with more under the bonnet than it should have had. I used it to drive round and suss out where the four coppers and one ex-Assistant Commissioner lived. I wanted to get to know them a little better. In their native habitat, as it were. I couldn't use my E-Type. It would have stuck out like a sore thumb and brought Collier back down on me like a ton of bricks.

Apart from Harvey, who lived in a scruffy-looking purpose-built flat between Lewes and Haywards Heath, they all looked like they were doing well.

I checked on Harvey's other daughter too: Jacqueline. She was the only one that I could talk to without landing myself in trouble. And I wasn't ready for any more trouble yet. Maybe never. But maybe I wouldn't have any choice in the matter.

I found that she'd left home when she was eighteen, and moved to London, where she was working as a copy typist and telephonist for a firm of commercial building surveyors in Gray's Inn, and lived alone in a tiny flat in Vauxhall.

I couldn't think of anything worse.

23

That is until I saw the office she worked in. It was in a faceless terrace off the Gray's Inn Road. I phoned the office in the afternoon and a bloke answered. Obviously Jacqueline Harvey was temporarily off the switchboard. Maybe she was doing a bit of copy typing. I asked what time the office closed, and he told me five-thirty. I put the phone down when he started asking me why I wanted to know.

I drove up in the Jag, and arrived at five-fifteen. At five-thirty on the dot, people started coming out of the front door. Five minutes later Jacqueline Harvey left. Even though I hadn't seen her for over twelve years, and she'd only been a child then, I recognised her straight away.

Her red hair was darker now, and the glass in her spectacles was thicker, but I knew it was her. She was tall, but the loose raincoat she wore gave no indication what her figure was like underneath it.

As she passed the car in the direction of the main road, I got out and followed her.

'Miss Harvey,' I said to her retreating back.

She almost jumped out of her coat as I spoke. She spun round, clutching her handbag tightly to her front. Her wrists were very thin and very white, with blue veins clearly visible beneath the skin.

'Sorry,' I said. 'I didn't mean to startle you.'

'Who are you?' she demanded. 'What do you want?'

Close up, her face was plain, devoid of any trace of make-up. But perhaps she wanted to be plain. There were too many frown marks on her forehead. And the grooves running down from the side of her nose to the corners of her mouth were too deep for someone so young. Almost as if she'd cultivated them in a warm, dark room.

'My name's Sharman,' I said. 'Nick Sharman. I knew your father.'

'How fortunate for you. Now what do you want?'

'It's about your sister.'

Her pale face became paler still.

'What about my sister?'

'About what happened to her twelve years ago.'

'What about it?'

'I worked on the case.'

'*What?*'

'I was one of the investigating officers at Brixton police station at the time.'

I thought she was going to hit me when I said that. Punch me in the face with all the strength in one of her skinny arms. I even went as far as to step back out of range, I was so convinced she was going to give me a right-hander.

'Then you know what happened, don't you?'

Our meeting was not going well. 'I'm a private detective now,' I said, and fumbled one of my cards out of my pocket and gave it to her. She glanced at it without looking.

'I'd like to talk to you about it,' I said.

'I have nothing to say.'

'I think it's important.'

She looked round, almost in panic. 'I should be getting home,' she said.

'It won't take long, I promise. Let me take you for a drink. I'll give you a lift home.'

She looked terrified at the thought of being alone in a car with me.

'Or get you a cab,' I added.

'I don't drink,' she said.

'A coffee?'

'Caffeine is a poison. I never touch it.'

'A soft drink. Perrier.'

She hesitated. 'Why do you want to talk to me about what happened?'

'The man who was convicted was released from prison recently.'

'I know that.' If I expected her to say that he should never have been set free, I was disappointed.

'He killed himself a couple of months ago.'

'Good riddance.'

'But I don't think he did what he went to prison for.'

Her face went even paler. So pale that I thought she was going to faint, and I put one hand out to steady her. 'No,' she said. 'No.' And I didn't know if she meant that I shouldn't touch her, or if she was denying what I was saying. Then with one more frightened look, she ran off towards the nearest bus stop where a Routemaster had just pulled up. She stood at the back of the crowd waiting to climb aboard, looking nervously at me in case I joined her.

I stood on the corner and watched as she boarded it and went inside the lower deck, and the bus pulled slowly away to join the stream of traffic heading towards Holborn.

24

She called me the next morning. 'Mr Sharman?' she said.
'Yes,' I replied. I didn't recognise her voice.

'It's Jacqueline Harvey here.'

I was surprised. 'Hello,' I said.

'I kept the card you gave me. I was thinking about what you said last night. I hardly slept.' She paused.

'Yes,' I said again.

'I've decided I will talk to you.'

'Good. When?'

'The sooner the better. Tonight?'

'I'm not doing anything.' The girls were working. An all-nighter, with everything that entailed.

'But it has to be somewhere private. Somewhere that we won't be disturbed,' she said.

'It's up to you,' I said. 'You choose. A restaurant. A bar. Whatever you want.' I didn't suggest her place. I didn't want her to have an inkling that I knew where she lived, or under what circumstances.

She hesitated. 'I said somewhere private,' she said. 'Not a public place.'

'That doesn't leave a lot of options.'

She hesitated again. 'Do you live alone?' she asked.

'Yes.'

'Where?'

'I have a flat in Tulse Hill.'

'Can I trust you?' she asked.

A stupid question really. I was hardly going to say no. But something in her voice told me that what she'd asked was not really what she wanted to know. That me arriving like that outside her office had triggered something inside her that had been lying dormant for a long time. 'Miss Harvey,' I said, 'I have no intentions of doing you any harm. I've got mixed up with something that started all those years ago when your sister was murdered.' The word 'murdered' hung between us like a dead fish, but I carried on. 'Believe me, if I felt I had any options I wouldn't have come looking for you last night. I know that you don't know me. But I promise you that all I want is the answers to a few questions. Nothing more. You can trust me. You have my word.'

Which, as I might have remarked on before, plus a quid will buy you a cup of coffee.

There was a pause. 'Give me your address,' she said. 'I'll come round later.'

I did as she requested. 'What time?' I asked.

'I finish work at five-thirty as you obviously know. I imagine I could be with you by six forty-five or so.'

'I'll make us a meal,' I said.

'There's no need for that.'

'I'd enjoy it. I don't often get the chance. Is there anything you don't like?'

If she'd said 'you', like I half expected her to, we might have laughed and got off to a better start. But she didn't. 'I eat most things,' was all she did say.

'Meat?' After the crack about caffeine, I thought there was a good chance she was vegetarian.

'Yes.'

'Steak?'

'That would be acceptable.'

'OK. I'll see you later,' I said.

'Goodbye,' she replied, and hung up her phone in my ear.

I took a walk down to Gateways, and picked up a pair of fillet steaks, and some lemon sorbet from the freezer. Then I went to the greengrocers next door and bought two big baking potatoes, the makings of a green salad, and the ingredients for my mother's recipe vegetable soup.

I returned home and started getting the meal together. I hadn't lied. It had been a long time since I'd cooked for anyone. Even someone as hostile as Jacqueline Harvey.

By six everything was ready. The soup was keeping warm on top of the stove. The potatoes were cooking away inside it. The steaks were peppered and buttered and sitting beneath the grill. The green salad was lying in a bowl on top of the tiny breakfast bar that I use as a dining table. The sorbet was in the freezer, and the coffee pot was full of decaffeinated. I'd bought a couple of bottles of wine on my way home. Just for me. And the spirits cupboard was stocked up full.

Perfect.

She rang my doorbell at six-fifty precisely. I went down and let her in. She was carrying a Thresher's off-licence bag that clinked attractively as she went up the stairs in front of me.

'I thought you didn't drink,' I said, as she handed it to me when we got inside my flat.

'Sometimes with a meal,' she said. 'It's for you mainly. As you're being kind enough to cook for me.'

'Do I look like I could drink two bottles of wine in an evening by myself?' I asked.

'Yes,' she replied. 'And you said you used to be a policeman. All policemen drink. I should know.'

I imagined she did.

I took her loose coat. Underneath it she was wearing a loose dress that also disguised her figure.

'Do you want some wine?' I asked.

'A little.'

'Please sit down.'

She chose the sofa, and I went off to get a pair of glasses and open one of the bottles of perfectly acceptable red wine that she'd brought with her.

I poured out two glasses, gave one to her, and took mine and perched on the edge of one of the two stools you have to sit on to eat in my place.

'Sorry it's a bit crowded in here,' I said, referring to the furniture that seemed to fill the place when there was more than one person present.

'It suits me,' she said. 'It's a bit like my place.'

'You live alone?' I asked.

She nodded.

'All alone,' she added unnecessarily, and sipped at her wine.

I thought I'd serve the first course before I got down to cases and busied myself with the soup.

She joined me at the breakfast bar and dug in. 'This soup is very good,' she said after the first mouthful.

'Mother's own,' I said. 'I learnt to cook it at her knee.'

'You don't look the type.'

'What type do I look, then?' I asked.

'Mr Macho. The type I detest.'

'Thanks,' I spluttered.

'Although I might be wrong,' she added.

When the soup was drunk, and before I put a light to the grill, I said, 'Why did you change your mind? About talking to me, I mean.'

'It was what you said last night.'

I gave her a quizzical look.

'About the man who was convicted for the murder of my sister being innocent.'

'I wouldn't go that far,' I said. 'But in this case I don't think he did what they said he did. And what he went to prison for.'

'What makes you say that?'

'I don't know really. I never ever thought that he did.'

'Why didn't you do something about it then? All those years ago.'

'It's a long story.'

'Tell me.'

So I told her. I told her about talking to Sailor the night Collier and Lenny had beaten him into giving a confession. About me being the new boy. Scared about jeopardising my job. Lacking in confidence. The whole nine yards.

'Typical,' she said.

I pulled a face. 'It goes with the job,' I said. 'You must know that. Don't upset the apple-cart. Play the game. Maintaining a solid front with your colleagues. All that sort of stuff.'

'I know,' she said. 'Only too well.'

I stood up and started cooking the steaks. She poured herself another glass of wine. A large one.

We ate mostly in silence. We finished the first bottle of wine with the main course and most of the second one. I was glad I'd got a couple of bottles of wine in too. For someone who didn't drink, Jacqueline Harvey was making a good stab at getting pissed.

When our plates were empty, I said, 'Miss Harvey.'

'Call me Jacqueline,' she said. 'No. Call me Jackie. No one's called me that for a long time.' And she gave me a stoned smile.

It was around then that I realised I might have bitten off a little more than I could chew.

And I didn't mean in the fillet steak department.

25

'OK,' I said. 'Jackie it is.'

'That's what my dad used to call me.'

I got up and opened another bottle of wine. 'Want some?' I asked. She nodded.

I filled her glass, took the dirty dishes over to the sink, removed the sorbet from the freezer and served it up.

'You're a very good host,' said Jackie.

'Like I told you, I don't get the chance too often these days.'

'I bet.' I noted a hint of flirtatiousness in her tone, and smiled.

We ate the sweet, and I leaned over and turned up the light under the coffee pot. 'No caffeine,' I said.

'You remembered.'

'The way you were so adamant about it, how could I forget?'

'I'm sorry if I was rude. Your turning up was something of a surprise.'

'I should have phoned first.'

'Then I probably wouldn't have seen you at all.'

'That's why I didn't.'

I removed the pudding dishes from the table and poured the coffee. It didn't taste bad but, knowing what it was, just a bit flat. Besides, I like caffeine.

'Do you mind if I smoke?' I asked.

'You're being very careful with me.'

'Yes, I suppose I am.'

'I'm not made of glass you know.'

'You give the impression you might be.'

'I don't mean to. Of course you can smoke. It's your flat.'

'You're my guest.'

'You're kind.'

'Not really.'

'You give the impression you might be.' She mimicked my tone, and we both laughed.

I got out the brandy bottle from the cupboard. 'Do you want some of this?' I asked. 'Being teetotal and all.'

'A little drop.'

I poured the liquor into two brandy balloons, and went back to my seat at the table.

'Do you have a girlfriend?' she asked.

I thought of Dawn and Tracey, and wondered what Jacqueline Harvey would make of them. 'Not really,' I said.

'What does that mean?'

'You'd have to define girlfriend.'

'That's a funny thing to say.'

'Not really.'

'You keep saying that.'

'Not really,' we both said together, and we laughed again. Things were looking up.

'Well, have you?' she pressed.

'What?'

'Got a girlfriend.'

'No one serious. Just some friends who happen to be girls. Women. Have you got a boyfriend?

'No.' It was definite. Emphatic.

I nodded.

'Are you surprised?'

'Nothing much surprises me these days.'

'I bet I could tell you something that surprises you.'

'What?'

'I've never kissed anyone.'

I thought I'd heard her wrong.

'What?' I said.

'I've never kissed anyone in my life,' she said.

What can you say to that?

'That surprises you doesn't it?' she asked.

I nodded.

'I told you I could. I could tell you other things that would surprise you too.'

'Like what?'

'I can't tell you…' Then she paused. She shook her head and smiled mysteriously, and somewhat tipsily. 'I've been kissed a few times,' she said. Going back to the previous subject. 'It was horrible. All wet and slimey.'

'If it's the right person it's OK,' I said.

She took off her glasses and put them on the table.

It was no 'Why, Miss Smith, you're beautiful' number, believe me. She wasn't, and that was a fact. Her face was pinched and plain, and without her bins she screwed up her eyes to see me, and I was only a couple of feet away.

'And of course I've never made love with anyone. Not after what happened to Carol. I just couldn't. What a pair, eh? No grandchildren for Daddy. And no great nieces or nephews for Uncle Alan. No fear of that. A 24-year-old virgin. What a joke. And poor Carol, who never even got to live to be twenty-four.'

'I'm sorry,' I said.

'You don't have to be.'

'I still am. I feel somehow responsible. I should have done a better job.'

'Caught the real murderer, you mean?'

This was a turn-up. 'You don't think that the man who went to prison did it either?' I said.

She didn't answer.

'Last night, when I told you that I was on the original investigation team, I thought you were going to hit me. Is that because you thought we'd got the wrong man too?'

She was silent.

'Jackie?' I said.

'Would it make any difference now, if the wrong man *had* gone to prison?'

Maybe it would to him, I thought. 'I suppose not,' I said. 'But you still haven't told me if you think that the wrong man *was* convicted.'

'Do we have to talk about it any more? It upsets me,' she said.

I didn't want her doing another runner. 'Not if you don't want to,' I said. Besides, I couldn't make her.

'I don't. I'm sorry, I haven't helped you much, have I?'

'I didn't expect you would. How could you? I just wanted… Christ, I don't know what I wanted.'

'Have you spoken to my father?'

'No.'

'Nor have I. Not for years. Carol being killed really smashed our family up. Not that it was much of a family before. Not since Mum died.'

'You really don't have to talk about it, you know,' I said.

'But I'm obsessed with it. Oh hell, can I have another drink?'

'Are you sure?'

'I'm not stupid. I may be the oldest virgin in bloody London, but I do know if I want a drink or not.'

'Brandy?' I asked.

She nodded.

She passed out on the sofa about eleven-thirty. I should have seen it coming, but I didn't. I wasn't too clever myself by then I must admit, and that's the only excuse I can offer.

I didn't undress her or anything. Just took her shoes off, put her feet up, tossed a blanket over her, and put a cushion under her head.

Then I threw the four empty wine bottles and the empty brandy bottle into the trash, put out the light, undressed and got into my own bed.

26

Jacqueline woke me up when she joined me. The digital read-out on the bedside clock read 3.08. Its tiny green figures were the only light I could see. The streetlamp outside my window was on the blink, and the room was pitch black.

She was naked except for her underpants. I was naked except for my shorts. She'd let her hair down and I felt it lying across my chest. She held me tightly, and I could feel her trembling. Neither of us said a word. I just moved slightly, the better to accommodate the weight of her on me.

I didn't do anything but lie there quietly. I knew it wasn't sex she wanted. No more than I did. It was just someone to hold. To be close to. She began to cry, and soaked the pillow and the sheet and my shoulder. I stroked her back after a bit. It was thin and boney, and I ran my fingers down her spine, feeling every cartilage in it as I did so.

When the clock read 3.54, and she seemed to be cried out, she said, 'I told you a lie.'

'What?' I said, and my voice was thick in the silence of the room.

'About being a virgin.'

'What about it?'

'I'm not.'

'You don't have to be.' I couldn't think of anything else to say.

'You don't understand.'

I didn't, to be honest.

'I've never made love. I didn't lie about that...' She paused.

'Tell me, Jackie,' I said. I knew that she would anyway. I just wanted to let her know that I wanted to hear.

She was silent again as the clock flickered to 3.55, then 3.56.

'It was Uncle Alan.' Her voice sounded younger. Almost girlish.

I'd nearly dropped off again during her silence. 'What?' I said. 'What did you say?'

'It was Uncle Alan,' she repeated.

I was suddenly wide awake. 'What was?'

'He did it.'

'Did what?'

'Fucked me.' Her voice wasn't girlish any more. It was as hard and cold as steel left out in a winter frost.

'Byrne. Your uncle?'

'That's what I said.' She was trembling harder by then. I wanted to turn on the light so that I could see her, but I didn't. I didn't want to break the mood she was in.

'Are you serious?' I asked.

I felt her breath on my face as she said, 'It's not something I'd joke about.'

I lay back and looked up in the direction of the ceiling, invisible in the darkness. Byrne. Of course. It fitted perfectly. Like a glove.

'Tell me,' I said.

So she did.

It was a sordid little story of constant child abuse. The constant abuse of Carol and Jacqueline Harvey. Ten and eight years old respectively when it had started. Just after their mother died.

It was the kind of story I'd heard lots of times before. The story of a trusted male relative left with young children. Tickling, touching, intimacy. Followed by isolation, violence, and finally violation. Then more tickling and touching when he needed the release again.

And finally threats and guilt. Not guilt by the violator, but by the violated.

It had gone on for years – four to be precise – and had culminated in the rape and murder of Carol Harvey one warm afternoon in Brixton.

'She threatened to tell Daddy,' Jacqueline whispered. 'Uncle Alan made her come and meet him that day. You know the rest.'

I knew all right. I remembered that day as clearly as any other in my life.

'But why did she go to see him alone? And on his ground? It was insane.'

I felt her shrug in the darkness. 'He had a power over us. Isn't that obvious? You don't recover from years of what he did to us overnight. And besides, he could be nice.' She paused. 'Isn't that sickening. Probably the most sickening part of all. In everything but the abuse he was a wonderful uncle. I can't believe I'm saying this, but he was. Sometimes we thought we were imagining it. Or that all adults did what he did to the children they looked after. Can you realise how that made us feel? But we just never dared ask. And besides, who knows what goes on in the minds of children? Because that's what we were. Even if we had to grow up fast.' There was a terrible desolation in her voice as she said those last words.

'I can't remember what we thought. I can't even remember what it's like to be a child. He stole that from us.'

I lay there for another minute and clasped her hand. Trying to give her some comfort, although there was precious little comfort to be had in the barren world she inhabited.

'Why didn't you tell anyone?' I asked finally. 'Afterwards, I mean.'

'I did.'

'What?'

'I did tell someone.'

'Who?'

'That man Collier. The detective sergeant.'

'When?'

'The day after it happened.'

'What did he do?'

'He took me in to see Uncle Alan.'

I felt sweat break out of every pore on my body in anger at what she was telling me. 'And what did *he* do?'

'He got rid of Collier. Told him it was my imagination. Then when we were alone, he told me he'd kill me if I ever breathed a word to another soul. That I'd end up like Carol.'

Simple as that, see. It doesn't take a lot to terrify a twelve-year-old girl whose sister had been raped the day before, and would die later that day. Especially when the person she went to for help just delivered her back to the perpetrator of the horror again.

'What happened then?'

'He called Collier back, and I told him what Uncle Alan had said was true. That I'd imagined it. That I was upset by what had happened.'

But I'd bet that Collier *had* believed her story. He had believed that Byrne had done exactly what she said he'd done. I'd stake my life on it. In that stinking flat on the Lion, I almost had.

'Did you ever tell your father?' I asked.

'No. It wouldn't have been any good. Uncle Alan would've just twisted it round again. No one would ever have believed me.'

'But you should have told him. Made him believe you.'

'I was frightened, Nick. Terrified. How could I tell my father that his brother-in-law was fucking both his daughters in the backside with that horrible thing of his.'

'He did that?' I said.

'Sometimes. He wasn't fussy. He had plenty of warm, wet holes to choose from between the two of us.'

I felt physically sick at what she was saying, and the way she said it. And I thought of my own daughter, and how I'd feel in similar circumstances.

'Before she was killed we decided to tell. That was what she was going to tell him we were going to do. Someone might have believed both of us together. But look what happened to her. That afternoon in the police station, I plucked up the courage to tell someone on my own, and look what happened to me.'

'I remember it,' I said. 'I was there. I saw you.'

'*You* were the one talking to Daddy. You went into an office together.'

'That's right.'

'That's when I told Collier. When you two were talking.'

'I remember the look on your face as you left. You looked…' I stopped. 'You looked as if your world had ended,' I said.

'It had.'

'Christ, Jackie,' I said. 'I wish you'd spoken to me.'

'I would have done. You looked kind. Not like the others. But you went off with Daddy. Anyway, even if I had, would you have believed I was telling the truth?'

'I would have tried to find out.'

She hugged me tighter. 'Would you? Against all those senior officers? And you the new DC? I'd like to believe you, Nick, but I'm not sure that I do. But thanks for saying it anyway.'

'Collier believed you,' I said.

'No.'

'Yes. Straight after you told him about your uncle, he and his mate Lenny Millar, with the collusion of a DI named Grisham, half killed Sailor Grant to get a confession. I was there some of the time. I couldn't handle it. That's why Grant went to jail. To protect your uncle. He was a flyer. Everyone in the job knew that. Look where he ended up. Just one stop from the biggest job of all in London. And that means the whole country. They could literally get away with murder with your uncle's collusion. Jesus! They almost did with me.'

'What?'

'Nothing. Forget it.'

'The bastards.'

'Jackie,' I said. 'You're going to have to tell now.'

'I know,' she said. 'Will you help me? I trust you.'

And those few simple words from someone who must have had all trust stolen from her years before were what started me crying too.

27

When we woke up the next morning, we were still in each other's arms, and I had a huge erection that was sticking through the material of my shorts into the soft flesh of her belly. We opened our eyes at exactly the same moment. It happens like that sometimes. I could actually see hers trying to focus through the gum that coated the lids. When they did and she realised where she was, she shot away from me over to the far side of the bed so fast that I thought she was going to keep going and fall on to the floor.

She tugged the sheets up to her throat, and said in a rusty little voice, 'What happened?'

'You got drunk,' I said. 'We got drunk,' I added.

She looked under the sheet at her nakedness. 'Did we... ?'

I shook my head, which was not a good idea, as it felt like my brain had got loose and was bumping from one side of my skull to the other.

'How come I'm here, then?' she asked.

'It was your idea,' I said in a voice that sounded equally as rusty as hers. 'I was the perfect gentleman.'

I saw realisation dawn on her face, still creased and puffy from sleep and too much alcohol.

'I told you, didn't I?'

I nodded. It occurred to me that communication by sign language was favourite until I'd had at least three cups of tea.

'And you believed me?'

I nodded again, then threw back the covers and got out of bed. Jacqueline averted her eyes. But at least my erection had subsided.

I took my robe off the back of the door and threw it to her; then I put on yesterday's T-shirt, and pulled on my jeans, went to the wreckage that had once been my kitchen, and stuck on the kettle.

'Tea?' I asked. 'Juice?'

'Juice please. I've got to use the bathroom. Don't look.'

I turned my back and heard the rustling as she got out of bed, pulled on the robe, and ran to the bathroom.

By the time she got back, the kettle had boiled, and I'd put a glass of mixed orange and grapefruit juice on the breakfast bar for her.

She drank it down greedily. She looked better, having combed her hair and washed her face. She found her glasses and put them on, sat on a stool and said, 'So what are you going to do?'

'Blow the whole thing open,' I said.

'After all this time?'

'Of course. Time doesn't matter. Not in a murder case.'

'How? Go to the police?'

'No. Better than that.'

'Tell me.'

I told her. I told her what I planned to do. I told her about the evidence I'd gathered and how it had led to her.

When I'd finished, I said, 'Of course it all hinges on you being prepared to tell the truth. It's not going to be easy. A lot of people are going to be hurt. A lot of important people. People dead, and people alive. Reputations are going to be ruined. There'll be pressure on you to deny that it happened. Can you handle that?'

'Yes,' she said, 'I can. I'm tired of living like this. Living a lie, and watching guilty people walk around free.'

'So do I do it?' I asked.

She nodded. 'Christ,' she said. 'What's the time?'

I found my watch. 'Ten to nine,' I said.

'I'm late. Sod it. I feel lousy. I'm going to go home and call in sick at work.'

'Good idea. Hangovers can get you real bad.'
'Especially if you've never had one before.'
'They don't get any easier,' I said.

28

Jacqueline got dressed and left, and I showered, shaved, put on clean clothes, and called Chas at the *South London*. He was at his desk.

'What can I do for you?' he asked.

'Keep your voice down to a dull roar, for a start,' I said. 'I'm suffering.'

'I hope it was a goodnight.'

'Depends what you call good. And it's what I can do for you.'

'Seems I've heard that song before.'

'You want a permanent job at Wapping, don't you?'

'Yeah.'

'I've got a story that'll guarantee it.'

'Tell me.'

'Not on the phone.'

'That good?'

'Plus.'

'Lunch?'

'When?'

'Today, if it *is* that good.'

I thought of the remains of the red wine and the brandy swilling around inside me, and one of Chas's lunches, and all that entailed, and my stomach almost rebelled. But there was no time like the present.

'How's the expenses?' I asked.

'*You* wanted to see me,' he said.

'Believe me, when you hear this, you'll beg to pay. And let's go somewhere quiet. I don't want the whole world and his wife listening in.'

'Let me think,' said Chas. 'Chinese – no. Indian – too heavy for lunch. Greek – you hate. Italian – too noisy. I know – how do you fancy West Indian cuisine? There's a good Caribbean restaurant opened up just round the corner.'

'Whatever,' I said.

'Right. West Indian it is. I'll book a table. One o'clock do you?'

'Fine.'

He gave me the name and address of the place and terminated the call.

I made more tea.

At twelve-fifteen, I wrapped the exercise book with the galleon on the cover in a brown paper bag, and took it and myself for a slow stroll to Streatham. I arrived at the restaurant ten minutes early. It looked OK from the outside, and I went in. A charming black woman checked the reservation, told me that I was the first to arrive, and led me to a table for two behind the sound-system speakers and a huge cheese plant that made it so private I might have been in my own front room. She recommended a frozen daiquiri, and I succumbed.

Mind you, it *was* damn good.

Chas turned up spot on time and joined me at the table. He ordered a similar drink; the waitress left the menus and went behind the bar to prepare it.

'You look rough,' he said.

'Thanks,' I replied. 'The next time I want to feel good about myself, I'll be sure to search you out.'

'Do that.'

His drink arrived and he said, 'What do you want to eat?'

'Christ knows.'

'Mind if I order for both of us?'

'Not at all.' Right then, I couldn't handle the responsibility of choosing a meal.

The waitress came back, and Chas ordered coconut soup to start; then for the main course: doctor fish, whatever the hell that was, chicken and rice, ackee, black-eyed peas in gravy, with a green salad on the side. It sounded enough to feed an army. But it was on his bill, so he could order what he wanted.

The waitress vanished again, and as we sipped our drinks Chas said, 'So what's this amazing story?'

'It's a long one.'

'I love long stories.'

Just then the soup arrived. It was laced with rum up to the legal limit and above, and its warmth finally began to make me feel better.

I started the story over the soup, and finished it over coffee and sweet rum liqueurs.

I told it to Chas in strict chronological order as I knew it. Starting the day of the rape, and ending with what Jacqueline had told me the night before.

'Christ,' said Chas, when I'd finished. 'That *is* a story.'

'Think the paper'll be interested?'

'I should say so. Just one thing though: I'm going to need corroborating evidence.'

I took the exercise book out of the bag and gave it to him. 'In there,' I said, 'are the present whereabouts of everyone involved – those that are still alive, that is. Plus everything I knew up until last night. Jacqueline Harvey knows I'm seeing you, and has agreed to talk to you about what happened. And I think there's something else. The piece of paper they talked about – if I just knew what it was and where it is. But I'll find out. Now, be careful, Chas. She and I are the only ones you can talk to. The others are dangerous. Except for Jackie's dad. He's just fucked up. If Collier and Millar learn what's going on, they might do to you what they did to me. Or worse. That's why I started investigating. I'm scared they'll come back one night and finish the job.'

I didn't mention what Collier had said about Dawn and Tracey. I didn't like to think too much about that.

'I always wondered what all that was about,' said Chas.

'Now you know. And do you want to know what the funniest

part of it is? If any of it's funny at all.'

'What?' he said.

'If Collier hadn't phoned me the night Sailor topped himself, none of this would be happening. I'd blanked him. I wasn't going to lift a finger to help him clear his name. If Collier had just thrown that letter away, I would probably never have known that Sailor was dead at all.'

'That's the way it goes.'

'Isn't it just?'

Chas sat and stared into space, but I knew exactly how his mind was working.

'So was it worth lunch?' I asked.

'I'll say.'

'Told you,' I said.

'Jee-sus,' said Chas. 'An Assistant Commissioner of the Met: a child abuser and a murderer. This is too much.'

'Isn't it?'

'You were right,' he said. 'This *will* get me the job I want.'

'Enjoy it,' I said as drily as I could.

'How much?' asked Chas.

'How much, what?' I said.

'How much do you want for the story?'

'Fuck off, Chas,' I said. 'I'm not interested in money.'

'You're the only one who isn't then.'

'Christ. You belong in fucking Wapping,' I said. 'With all the rest of the cheque-book journalists.'

'How about Jacqueline Harvey? Would she be interested?'

'Fuck knows, I don't,' I said.

He took a Vodafone from his inside pocket and switched it on. 'Sorry,' he said. He punched in a number, then said, 'Bob. Chas. Listen, I'm tied up here. Can you cover for me this afternoon?'

He paused. 'Nothing much. Just an interview with that bloke who found those bodies buried on his allotment. You'll do it? Great. I owe you one. Yeah, and I need some time off.' Another pause. 'Course it's important. Would I ask if it weren't? I can? You're terrific. I'll be in day after tomorrow. See ya.'

He killed the phone then punched in another number. 'Give me Tom Slade,' he said, when it was answered. Then, after a moment's pause, 'Tom. Chas Singleton. Listen, I've got a story here you'll kill for.'

He paused.

'It's a biggun'. I don't want to talk about it on the phone. It could be dangerous for several people, including me. Can I come in tomorrow before lunch and see you?'

Another pause.

'Great. See you.' He switched off the phone again and put it back in his pocket.

He winked at me, and called for more liqueurs. 'Great stuff, Nick,' he said. 'I think we've got a goer here.'

29

I called Jacqueline Harvey the same afternoon.

'He went for it,' I said, referring to Chas. 'Mind you, he's got to convince the hard-nosed editor of a national Sunday tabloid yet. But I think he'll do it. If he can't, no one can.'

'I hope so,' she replied. 'In fact, I'm counting on it.'

Me too, I thought, but didn't say so.

'When and if he does,' I said, 'he's going to need to have a long talk to you. I mean a really long talk, with everything going down on tape. Now, I know you told me, but he's not me. Is it still all right with you?'

'I told you I wasn't made of glass. I'll be fine.'

'No second thoughts?'

'None.'

'Good.'

'But I'd like you to be there when I do it. It's not going to be easy, not after all this time, and I need someone on my side.'

'You will have. Myself and Chas both. I'll be staying in close touch.'

'You're very thorough, Mr Detective.'

'I could have been more thorough at the start of all this,' I said. But I didn't want to go into all that again.

'Listen,' I said. 'Whatever happens, we've got to keep this close to our chests. I don't want Collier and his mates catching on to what we're doing. They play dirty, believe me; I've had more than enough experience of that. And there's more of them than there are of us. And they've got the might of the Metropolitan Police behind them. So don't tell anyone, and I mean *anyone*, what we're up to.'

'I understand. I haven't got anyone to tell anyway. And don't forget I've had experience of them too. Probably more than you.'

It was debatable, but I let it go.

'Sorry,' I said. 'I wasn't thinking.'

'That's all right.'

'We'd better meet soon, and discuss strategy. When are you free?'

'I'm not exactly overburdened with social engagements at the moment; I can probably fit you in when you want.'

I was beginning to get to like Jacqueline Harvey.

'Let me call you soon,' I said. 'I'll wait to hear from Chas first. When I hear something positive, we'll get together, OK?'

'Sounds good.'

'I'll buy you a drink after work one evening,' I said.

'I don't –'

'Don't say you don't drink,' I interrupted. 'I know better.'

'Can we keep it our secret?' she asked.

'Sure,' I said. 'My lips are sealed.'

And that was how we left it.

The next afternoon, Chas called me up at home. 'It's a good 'un,' he said. 'The news editor lapped it up. He's talking front page. But only if we can come up with some hard evidence. What you've given us so far is great. But he's scared of the libel lawyers. He'd be taking a big chance printing anything on what we've got right now.'

'Fair enough,' I said. 'I've spoken to Jacqueline Harvey. She's agreed to tell you everything. But she's a bit nervous. She wants me there when you do the interview. Is that OK with you?'

'The more the merrier,' said Chas. 'But I've got to do some ferreting of my own first. It's Thursday today. I'm going to have a dig around. Speak to some people I know. I'll talk to you if I come up with anything. All right?'

'You're the boss,' I said. 'But remember what I said, Chas. When you're out ferreting, just be careful. These boys play for keeps.'

'So do I,' he replied. 'Talk to you soon.'

I phoned Jacqueline at work and told her what Chas had said.

'That's good,' she said.

I agreed with her, and promised to let her know when I'd heard more from my pet reporter.

I felt a whole lot better after Chas's call and my brief chat with Jacqueline, both mentally and physically. At long last I thought that I was finally going to lay the ghost of Sailor Grant, and a whole load more besides.

The less ghosts there are in your life, the better it is, I figured.

But some ghosts just won't lie down.

Chas called me on Saturday afternoon.

'Christ,' he said. 'What kind of police force runs this town?'

'What do you mean?' I asked.

'I've seen a few contacts. Called in some favours. Been told a lot of stories. It seems that your mates Collier and Millar are well known.'

'Yeah?' I wasn't so sure I wanted to hear.

'Yeah. Seems like they've had *carte blanche* to do exactly as they please for the last decade or so. They've settled down in Peckham running a two-man private police force that can get away with pretty much what it wants.'

'Like?'

'Like copping backhanders from local businesses. Taking care that whores don't get nicked, for a nice lump of their profits. Protecting drug dealers from prosecution. Likewise for a nice cut. You name it, those two boys have got a finger in it. Literally in the case of some of the brasses. Apparently, if there's ever any complaints, someone with a lot of clout comes to their rescue like the Lone Ranger.'

'It's nothing more than I expected,' I said. 'I hope you've kept your head down.'

'Sure I have. I'm not silly, am I?'

'I hope not, Chas, for your sake,' I said.

'Trust me. I'm going to get some rest now. I've been up since

Thursday night. I'll talk to you Monday, OK?'

'Fine,' I said. 'Just take it easy. Remember what I said.'

'I will,' he replied and hung up.

I got straight on to Jacqueline. Apparently she'd just come back from Sainsbury's with the weekend shopping. I told her what Chas had told me.

'Is that good?' she asked.

'Not bad,' I said. 'Not bad at all. It pretty well confirms what I thought was happening. It makes our case stronger, which *is* good.'

'It is, isn't it?' she said.

'Yeah,' I agreed. 'I'll talk to you again when I've spoken to Chas on Monday. Take care.'

We said our farewells and I put down the phone.

On Sunday evening, Dawn came round by herself. I was getting to rely on her more and more as that year trundled towards its close. She was different with me when we were on our own than she was when anyone else was around. I felt sorry for Tracey. No, not sorry, but sad. I could see a chapter in both their lives ending. I think it would have happened whether I'd come along or not. I'd just been the catalyst. It was obvious that Dawn wanted to get back to the straight life.

Christ knows why. What had the straight life ever done for her?

Anyway, she came round. She bought a Chinese takeout: chop suey and chow mein, with a side order of ribs and a portion of fried rice.

I supplied the soy sauce.

We sat and ate the food out of the tin foil containers it came in, with the plastic chopsticks the restaurant supplied, and fought over the last rib.

We talked about what Chas had told me, and what had happened on the Lion the night I'd been beaten up, which was pretty depressing, and she talked some more about the babies she wanted to have. I didn't want to disillusion her, but the thought of changing nappies again didn't exactly fill me with the joys of spring.

We ended up in bed together, just like in the storybooks. A

paperback novel, where everything always works out in the end.

Not tonight, Josephine.

The bell to my flat rang at about two a.m. I came awake straight away, looking up into the darkness, with only the sound of Dawn's breathing disturbing the silence of the room, and I wondered if I'd imagined the noise. Then it rang again, ragged and urgent in the quiet of the night.

I got out of bed, pulled on T-shirt and jeans and went barefoot down the stairs. I didn't want to open the door, but I did. Chas was leaning against the porch wall outside. His face was a bloody mask, and as I pulled the door towards me he collapsed into my arms. He was such a dead weight that I almost dropped him. As it was he slid halfway down my body before I caught him securely, and he left a trail of blood down the cotton of my shirt, like a long red tyre track.

I held him up and it wasn't just his face that was a mess. He'd been given a right going over by the looks of it, and I would have put money then and there on who'd given it to him.

I sat him down in the hall with his back to the wall, and ran upstairs to call an ambulance. Dawn was coming to and I told her what had happened, but all she seemed to take in was the stains on my shirt.

The ambulance arrived twenty minutes later. Not bad. Poor Chas was mumbling and moaning and thrashing around on the floor by then, and a couple of times I had to hold him down as he tried to get to his feet. I asked him what had happened, but I might as well have been talking to myself. Perhaps I was.

I went with him to King's. At the rate I was going, pretty soon I'd have a life membership to casualty. A gold card.

The staff there wanted to know what had happened. I didn't enlighten them. When they took Chas away for X-rays, I stood outside in the chill night air and smoked a couple of cigarettes I'd bummed off the charge nurse.

Eventually a doctor came out to find me.

'Your friend took a pretty bad beating,' he said. 'Have you informed the police?'

That was a hoot. If Chas hadn't taken the hammering *from* a couple of the thin blue line that is all that stands between us and anarchy, I was a monkey's uncle. And I didn't have any brothers or sisters. Not any more.

'No,' I replied. 'I don't know what happened. He just turned up on my doorstep like that.'

'Well, take my word for it,' said the doctor who scowled at the cigarette I was holding, 'he didn't get those injuries by walking into a door.'

'Can I see him?' I asked.

'Out of the question. He's under sedation. He might even need surgery.'

'Tomorrow?' I asked.

'You can always try,' said the doctor, and he turned on his heel and left me alone.

I went back home by cab.

On the way, I decided to go out and get some form of protection for myself.

30

When I opened the flat door, Dawn was sitting on a stool at the breakfast bar, drinking coffee and inhaling a Silk Cut. She got up, dropped the cigarette into her coffee mug, where it died with a hiss, and came over and gave me a hug. Boy, did I need one.

'What happened?' she asked.

I let her know what I *thought* had happened. That Chas had stuck his beak into Collier and the rest's business just a bit too far, and they'd snapped it off.

'Will he be all right?'

I told her that I was none the wiser. The way I said it set her off. 'Oh God. He's not going to die is he?'

I took her in my arms and tried to comfort her. 'Relax,' I said. 'He'll be OK.'

As we stood together, taking some comfort in the warmth from each other's bodies, the phone rang. 'That's the fourth time,' said Dawn. 'When I answer it there's no one there. I thought it was you from a dodgy call box.'

I picked up the receiver, and said hello.

'You and your fucking mates never learn do they?' It was Collier.

'You cunt,' I said.

'Flattery will get you nowhere,' he replied. 'I told you, didn't I?

But you wouldn't listen. Fancy sending some bastard from the press around to do your dirty work.'

'You're fucked,' I said. 'It's just a matter of time.'

'Fucked for what?'

'For covering up for Byrne. I know what he did to Carol Harvey. And I know what you and Millar and Grisham did to cover it up.'

It was the first time I'd told Collier what I knew, but it didn't seem to worry him at all. He'd had too many years of being a law unto himself, and he took it in his stride. But I realised I'd probably signed my death warrant by telling him. 'Prove it,' he said coolly.

That was the problem: proof. But I knew that Collier had something hidden away somewhere. And it was my job to find it.

'I will,' I said.

'Don't hold your breath. It was all too long ago.'

'There's no time limit on murder.'

'I'm shaking in my shoes.'

'You will be.'

'Save it. Pull out now before someone gets seriously hurt.' He put down the phone.

'Who was that?' said Dawn.

'Collier.'

'He never gives up, does he?'

'He will. I'm going to have that bastard. I know he's got something that implicates Byrne. I've just got to find it.'

'Where?'

'His place. That's where I'll start. But right now I want you out of here. Somewhere safe. Not home. And get Tracey on the blower. I want her out of there too, as fast as she can go. Have you got someplace to go?'

'I don't want to leave you,' she said.

'I know you don't, but you've got to. It's too dangerous for you to be about. I've got enough things to think about without worrying about you.'

'We could go to Tracey's mum's.'

'Where's that?'

'Milton Keynes. They moved her up there when they knocked

down the old buildings in Bermondsey, where she used to live.'

'Terrific,' I said. 'Who'd ever think of looking for you *there*? Go on, phone Tracey up. I want you out of here now.'

'Nick, it's not six yet.'

'The best time. Tell her to get packed. Nip round and pick her up, and don't let anyone follow you.'

She began to protest, but I cut her off, and she did as she was told.

Dawn didn't say much when she got through, but I heard the urgency in her voice, and I hoped Tracey did too.

When she put down the phone, she said, 'I'm meeting her on the corner of our street in twenty minutes. She's packing us a bag each. She'll suss out if anyone's watching. She's an expert, is our Trace. Used to do a bit of hoisting. She's got eyes in the back of her head.'

Obviously Tracey had talents even I hadn't seen.

'Go on then,' I said. 'And be careful.'

She grabbed her handbag and left, pausing just long enough to rub her crotch against mine, and stick her tongue in my mouth.

'I'll be seeing you,' she said.

'Count on it.'

She went downstairs, and I heard the engine of her car start with a sound like pebbles being rattled in a cocoa tin. When the noise had faded, I rang Jacqueline Harvey. She answered on the tenth ring, just when I was beginning to get worried.

'Jackie,' I said, 'are you OK?'

'I was until you called at this ridiculous hour,' she complained.

I explained what had happened to Chas.

'Oh, no,' she said. 'It's starting again, isn't it?'

I didn't bother saying that it already had.

'The poor man,' she went on. 'All because of me. I hope he'll be all right.'

'So do I,' I said.

'Who did it?'

'Collier.'

'The policeman?'

'The same.'

'Can't you tell someone?'

'Who? The police? Don't make me laugh, Jackie. It doesn't work like that in the real world. They stand by their own. I've got no proof, at least until Chas comes to, and even then it's just his word against theirs.'

'This is a nightmare.'

'Tell me about it. Now I want you out of sight. Somewhere away from home. Is there anywhere you can go?'

'Not really. Anyway, why should I go anywhere? I haven't done anything wrong.'

'I know that,' I said patiently. 'But I still think you'd be better off away. Haven't you got any friends you could visit for a few days?'

'No.'

'How about your father?'

'I haven't seen him for ages. I told you that.'

'I think it might be time for a tearful reunion. I believe he's living near Lewes these days.'

'That's right. Did I tell you that?'

'Someone did. Please. I'd feel much happier if you were down there with him, rather than up here on your own.'

'I'm not going there.'

'You'd be safer.'

'Is that right? I haven't felt safe around the male members of my family for a long time. My father did nothing to protect my sister and myself all those years ago. Why would I be safe with him now?'

'Your father didn't know what was going on,' I said.

'He should have made it his business to know.'

Which was fair enough.

'I could stay with you,' she said.

The silence hung heavy over the line.

'No,' I said.

I heard her exhale breath. 'Don't worry, I'm not after your manly body.'

'That's not the problem, Jackie,' I replied. 'The problem is that here you're as much a hostage to fortune as you are at your own place. I'd love for you to stay, believe me. I wish it was that simple.

But I want you somewhere out of the way. Not in the main combat zone, which it looks like this flat is fast becoming.' I thought for a moment. 'How about a hotel?' I said.

There was another, longer pause.

'I suppose,' she said.

'I'll get something fixed up. I'll talk to the news editor on the paper. Maybe they'll help. Otherwise I'll book you something myself. Could you go this morning?'

'No. I have to go to work. I can't just vanish. I need to give them a little notice.'

'How much?'

'If I go in today, maybe I could take some time off, starting tomorrow.'

'That sounds good. Do it as soon as you go in. I'll call you later.'

'All right.'

And with that we made our farewells.

Straight away I called the offices of the paper Chas was writing the story for. It was still not six-thirty, but the switchboard was open, and the woman who answered told me that Tom Slade wouldn't be in until eight. I said I'd ring back.

Then I made some tea, lit a cigarette, and sat down to have a good think.

I was still sitting there an hour later with an ashtray full of cigarette ends, a cup half full of cold PG Tips with a skin on the top, and a mouth that tasted like an open sewer, when the doorbell rang.

I stayed where I was and it rang once more. Shit, I thought, not again.

I went over to the window, pulled back the edge of the curtain and squinted through the gap. There was a dark blue Sierra that I didn't recognise parked behind my Vauxhall. It had an RT aerial stuck to the back window and screamed Old Bill.

I went downstairs as the doorbell rang for the third time. I took the sawn-off pool cue I keep in the kitchen in case of mice with me.

I decided that if it was Collier, I was going to hit him first and ask questions later. Maybe not the wisest thing to do under the circumstances, but certainly the most satisfying. I flung open the door and Detective Inspector Robber was standing inside the porch gnawing on an apple.

'Elevenses?' I said.

He tossed the core into the front garden and pushed past me. 'You took your bleeding time,' he said. 'I'm dying for a piss. And put that thing down. It's an offensive weapon, and I could nick you for carrying it.' He lumbered up the stairs to my flat.

I followed him up, and walked through the door behind him, put the pool cue back where it belonged and cleared away the cup and ashtray as I heard him relieving himself into my toilet.

When he came out, I said, 'You didn't wash your hands.'

He didn't reply, just took one of my cigarettes from the open packet and lit it with one of my matches, then sat down.

'Make yourself at home,' I said.

Still no reply.

'I suppose you want tea?' I said.

He nodded.

'Have you got this place mixed up with a café and public convenience?' I said.

He snorted.

'Is this official?' I always seemed to be asking him that.

'What do *you* think? You turn up at King's in the middle of the night with a reporter who looks like he's gone six rounds with the Terminator. Then I come round, and I'm greeted with you wielding a bloody club like a caveman out to catch his lunch, and you ask me if it's official. Course it's bloody official. And you're lucky it's me that's doing the asking, otherwise you'd be down at the station, not making tea here. And talking of that, get it brewed, will you, I'm gasping.'

I went into the kitchen and pushed the button on the back of the electric kettle, pulled out two mugs, and put in tea bags, milk and sugar.

Robber stubbed out the cigarette and lit another.

'So what's the story?' I asked.

'That's what I was hoping you'd tell me.'

I shrugged, as the kettle boiled, and I filled the mugs and stirred them.

'Don't fuck about for *Christ's* sake,' said Robber. 'I've only got so much patience.'

I told him what had happened: Chas arriving on the doorstep and me getting him to the hospital. That was all I was going to tell him.

'And what do you think brought it all on?' asked Robber.

'I don't know,' I lied.

'It's just coincidence I suppose,' he said with heavy irony. 'You're beaten up a few weeks ago, and now your mate gets the same treatment. A reporter who everyone knows is as thick as thieves with you.'

'It's a tough town,' I said. 'These things happen.'

I took his mug over to him and he looked up at me. 'Don't take the piss, Sharman. What do you think I've got for brains here? Cold rice pudding? I've got a feeling you're obstructing my investigation, and I don't like that one little bit.'

'I don't know what you want me to say,' I replied.

'Just tell me who's behind all this, that's all. And why it's happening.'

'I wish I could,' I said.

And I did, sincerely. In fact, just for one second, I was tempted to tell Robber what was happening, but I knew that coppers' loyalty was thicker than water, so I didn't.

Robber snorted and gave me a right how's-your-father look.

'It wasn't me, you know,' I said. 'Who done it, I mean. I don't know why you're sitting here wasting time and taxpayers' money, and using my place like the staff canteen. Why aren't you out finding the real villains?'

I could tell Robber wasn't impressed by my earnest show of innocence. In his place neither would I have been.

I shut up then, for a minute.

'How is Chas?' I asked, after the minute was up. All the time I'd been sitting alone in my flat since Dawn had left, I'd been meaning to call the hospital, but I didn't have the nerve. Just in case the news was all bad.

'I thought you'd never ask,' said Robber. 'He'll survive. Just about. He's been badly beaten. By experts, the doctor says. His car's still outside where he lives. So whoever did it must have dumped him here. I wonder why that was?'

I shrugged again. What else could I do? But I knew each shrug was putting me on to thinner ice.

Robber slurped at his tea and lit a third cigarette. Come to think of it, I'd never ever seen him with a packet of his own.

When he'd drained the mug, he stood up and said, 'If you think of anything, give me a call. I'm not hard to find.'

Just hard to get shot of, I thought.

As if to ram home the point, he said, 'I'll be back. I know you're not giving me the full SP. You'll never bloody learn, Sharman, will you? You and your little one-man band. Why don't you just get into the real world and tell me what the fuck's going on, and save yourself and your mates any more grief?'

'If I could, I would,' I said. And once again I wasn't lying.

But Robber just shook his head sadly and left.

By then, it was past eight, and I rang the paper back. 'Tom Slade,' I said when the switchboard answered.

This time I got put through to his secretary who didn't like it when I refused to tell her who I was. Eventually a voice barked in my ear, 'What?'

'I'm a friend of Chas Singleton's,' I said. 'Have you heard?'

The bark dropped a decibel or ten and said, 'Yes. What kind of friend?'

'The friend who put him on to the story that might have put him where he is now.'

'The detective?'

'Correct.'

'Was it you that took him up to the hospital?'

'Right again.'

'Well I'm glad you did. What can I do for you?'

'Are you still investigating the story?'

'Yes.'

I breathed a sigh of relief.

'Chas was going to interview the young woman who broke it to me.'

'Yes.'

'I take it someone still is.'

'You take it right.'

'She's vulnerable. I need to get her somewhere safe. I'm worried she's going to end up where Chas is. She can't stay at her place, or mine, and she won't go to her father's. Apparently there's nowhere else. I want to put her into a hotel or a safe house. I thought you might know somewhere. You must be used to this sort of thing.'

'I am,' said Slade. 'Whereabouts is she?'

'London. She lives in Vauxhall, works in Gray's Inn.'

'Give me your number, and five minutes, and I'll come back to you.'

I gave him my phone number, put down the receiver and lit a cigarette. Before it was finished the phone rang again. It was Slade.

'The Fortescue in Bayswater,' he said. 'It's not bad. Three star. She's booked in as Miss Clancey from any time today. Stay indefinite. We pick up the tab. Does that suit?'

'Excellent,' I said. 'I'll get her there this evening. And I think you and I should meet.'

'I agree,' he said. 'Wait one, I need to check my diary.' He was gone for less than half a minute. 'I can't meet you before tomorrow noon. Is that all right?' he asked.

'It's fine with me.'

'Do you know the Crown & Sceptre in Titchfield Street?'

'Great or Little?'

'Great.'

'I'll find it.'

'Tomorrow at twelve then. Ask for me behind the bar.'

'I'll do that,' I said, and pressed down the cut-off button on the phone and called Jacqueline Harvey straight off. I caught her as she was leaving for work.

'I've got you a place to stay,' I said. 'The paper's fixed it up. They're still checking out the story.'

'Fine,' she said. 'Where is it?' She didn't sound that bothered, and it rather pissed me off.

'I'd rather not say,' I said.

'Oh, Nick, aren't you rather over-dramatising all this?'

'No, I'm not,' I said. 'You didn't see Chas last night or, for that matter, me a couple of months ago. And remember what happened to Carol?'

I could have bitten my tongue out. That was taking things a little too far.

'Jackie,' I said quickly, 'I'm sorry. Really sorry. I didn't mean to say that. I'm just terribly concerned.'

Her voice was quieter when she answered. 'I understand, Nick. But I would like to know. I won't tell anyone. I promise.'

So, against my better judgement, I told her.

'I'll pick you up from your office tonight,' I said. 'I'll run you home, wait while you pack a bag, and get you to the hotel. I'll see you snug in there, then I have an errand of my own to run.'

'All right,' she said. 'I'll see you at five-thirty, outside the office.'

'Fine,' I said, and hung up.

Now all I needed was a gun and a burglar.

31

First the burglar. And I needed a good one. I knew just the man. Or the Mann as it happened. 'Monkey' Mann to be precise. Cat burglar of this or any parish if not currently doing bird at Her Majesty's pleasure. A real pro. A peterman of the old school, who'd earned his nickname by climbing walls like a chimp on speed. I'd felt his collar a few times in the past, and now I used him if I ever needed a little second-storey work. He hung out at any one of twenty or so boozers in Beckenham, and I found him in the saloon bar of the Three Tuns, off the high street, just after opening, enjoying a large Irish whiskey and furrowing his forehead over the *Sun* crossword.

'Don't strain your brain, Monkey,' I said as I arrived at his table.

He looked up, startled. 'Blimey, Mr S,' he said. 'You gave me quite a fright.'

'You're getting old, Monkey,' I remarked, 'if that's all it takes these days.'

He grinned. He *was* getting old. His dark hair was thinning over his scalp and there were deep crevices in his skin where once there had only been the suggestion of worry lines. 'It comes to us all, don't it? You're looking a bit pale yourself. Been ill?'

'Something like that. How's business?'

'Not what it was. But what is?'

'I might have something for you. Want a drink?'

'Have I ever refused? Large Irish.'

I went to the bar and got Monkey his drink and a pint for myself. I took them back to the table and sat in the hard chair opposite his.

He sipped at the drink I'd bought him and asked, 'So what's the deal?'

I explained that I wanted to break into a bent copper's gaff. I told him that I didn't know what I was looking for exactly, and that it might not even exist. But if it did exist, and it wasn't in a safe-deposit box in a bank somewhere, then it was in the house.

'A safe, Mr S,' said Monkey wisely. 'That's what we're looking for.'

I also told him that Collier mustn't know he'd been paid a visit, which didn't worry Monkey one iota. He didn't even ask why, which was good. Because I didn't want to tell him that Collier would kill us if he ever found out.

'A bent copper's house,' he said. 'That sounds like a lark. Serves him right. Bastard.' Monkey thought all coppers were bent. It went with his territory. 'All belled up is it? The drum?'

I described Collier's little end-of-terrace house, and what I'd seen when I'd checked out the place on one of my visits. A Telecom alarm box over the door, complete with blue light.

'Ground-floor entry,' he said. 'That's good. But I'll have to go and have a squint meself, Mr S. I'll use the old window-cleaner trick. I expect the alarm will go through to the local nick, if it's Telecom like you said. His nick is it?'

I nodded.

'He'll be popular with the woodentops. They'll be missing their tea, having to go out to his gaff and answer a false alarm.'

'You're going to set it off?'

'Best thing. Alarms are notorious for being faulty. And the more hi-tech they are, the more faulty they tend to be.'

'But it won't be faulty, will it?'

'They'll think it is. Leave it to me, Mr S.'

I almost expected him to tell me not to worry my pretty little head about it, but he didn't dare. 'So we can get in and out, and no one any the wiser? Not even the engineer who comes to look for the non-existent fault?' I said, to be sure.

'*Mr S.*' He sounded offended that I might question his expertise.

'Sorry, Monkey,' I said. 'I was forgetting how good you are.'

'So what's in it for me?'

'A grand for a night's work.'

He didn't argue. He knew me better. 'Sounds all right. Any chance of a sub?'

I could read him like a book. Before I'd left home I'd put two hundred and fifty nicker into an envelope. I took it out and slid it across the table. He counted the money without looking, and grinned again. 'It has to be night-time,' he said. 'For maximum annoyance to the neighbours. What night suits you?'

'It's got to be soon.'

'First night he's out then. I'll check the place out today. Does he work nights, your copper mate?'

'Bound to.'

'Can you find out when he's next liable to be out all night?'

'Sure.'

'Give me his address, and I'll get back to you pronto,' he said.

I had the information on a separate sheet of paper, which I gave to Monkey, told him to ring me before five, bought him another Irish and left.

I called Peckham nick as soon as I got in and asked for Collier. I laid on the cockney accent to the max. I did the same when I got through to CID. The copper who answered didn't bother asking my name. He smelled fresh-cut grass, just like I wanted him to. 'He's not in today,' he said.

'How about tonight?' I grunted.

'Yeah. He's on nights this week.'

'T'riffic,' I said. 'I'll catch him later.' Literally, I hoped.

I smiled as I put down the phone. Perfect, I thought. Now it was down to Monkey.

He belled me at four. 'No probs, Mr S,' he said. 'It's just like I thought it would be. The locks on the front door are the business. Round the back they're a piece of shit. And the back door's sheltered by the walls of the garden. You could have a bunk-up round there and no one could see. And he *has* got a safe in there. I could smell it.'

'Terrific.' If Monkey said there was a safe inside the house, there was. The man's instinct was phenomenal. 'Can we get past the alarm?'

'A piece of piss. It'll take a while, but we'll get it sorted.'

'How?'

'You'll see.'

'And no one sussed you?'

'Get out of it.' Once again he sounded offended. 'I even earned a tenner on the windows. When can we do it? Tonight? Tomorrow?'

'I've got another errand to run tonight,' I said. 'Don't know how long it'll take. Tomorrow's good. He's working nights this week.'

'Tomorrow it is then. By the way, the cash is COD, ain't it?'

'Don't worry, Monkey. You'll get your money.'

'I know I will, Mr S. I trust you. Always have. It's just that I fancy a couple of days with the gee-gees next week and the rest of the dosh would come in handy.'

'It's as good as in your hand.'

'Right, I'll borrow a motor and pick you up about half-twelve tomorrow night. Sound all right?'

'Suits me. And *borrow* a motor?'

'It's kosher, Mr S. Don't fret. All being well it'll be back before the owner knows it's gone. I'll even stick some petrol in.'

'You're a good neighbour, Monkey.'

'Too right I am. Be at your window. I'll flash me lights. I don't want to knock on your door when I arrive.'

'Do I bring anything?'

'Just yourself,' he said. 'And the seven hundred and fifty nicker.' And he hung up.

32

Jackie Harvey was waiting on the pavement outside her office when I arrived to collect her, and I drove to Vauxhall and then on to Bayswater through a fine drizzle. The hotel was off Queensway and not difficult to find. We went into reception and checked in. The receptionist told us there was someone waiting for Miss Clancey, and indicated a straight-looking geezer with a beautiful head of blond hair, wearing a neat blue suit, sitting in an armchair by the door to the bar. I told Jackie to wait, and walked over to him not knowing what to expect. He came to his feet at my approach in the way that athletes do when they don't want to appear too athletic, and I wished that I was armed. At times like this I felt almost naked without a gun. I stopped just out of his reach, and he said, 'Mr Sharman?'

I didn't reply, but he must have seen my look.

He put out his hands in a gesture of surrender.

'Don't worry, sir,' he said politely, in an accent that was pure Eton and Oxford. 'Mr Slade sent me. I'm with the firm. I'm just going to reach into my side jacket pocket for my credentials.'

He did exactly that and passed me a leather wallet. Inside was a plastic laminate with his photograph, his name, which was Toby Gillis, and his job description. 'Security', it read. Nothing else, except that he had access to all areas inside any building within the publishing group.

'Sorry to give you a jolt,' he said. 'Mr Slade thought it might be a good idea for me to be around, just in case. Is that the young lady?' He indicated Jackie with his eyes.

'That's her,' I said. 'You don't mind if I ring Slade just to confirm?'

'I'd be disappointed if you didn't. There's a public phone over there.' This time his eyes moved round to my left. 'You do have the number?'

'I can remember it, thanks,' I said, and went over and quickly dialled the paper. I saw Jackie looking at me, and put up my hand to forestall her. I got put straight through to Slade's extension.

'Sharman,' I said. 'Toby Gillis. One of yours?'

'Hello, Sharman,' Slade said. 'Certainly. I meant to tell you I'd put one of our boys in. He's got the next room to Miss Harvey. I didn't know if you'd be staying.'

'I'm not,' I said. 'I have a few things of my own to sort out. It's a good idea.'

'He'll be there as long as she is. He's very discreet.'

'So I noticed,' I said. 'I hope he's as good.'

'He is. Take my word.'

'I've got no choice. But I'm glad he's here. She's checked in, and I'm leaving now.'

'Fine. I'll see you tomorrow then.'

'I'll be there,' I said, and hung up.

I went over to Jackie and explained who Toby Gillis was, then beckoned him over and introduced him to her. He was very polite.

Jackie asked me to stay for dinner, but I begged another appointment, and agreed to take a raincheck on dinner until the following evening. Gillis said that it would be his pleasure to keep her company. She shrugged, and said it was OK with her.

I wished them both a goodnight, and went back to the car and drove off in search of something to make me feel a little less naked.

33

Buying a gun in south London is not difficult. You just need to know where to go and who to see. And of course you need cash.

I went to a pub off the Falcon Road in Clapham Junction. I arrived at about eight on that miserable rainy evening and the pub was almost deserted.

I took a grand with me, split into ten bundles of a hundred pounds each, and stashed away separately in the pockets of my jeans, shirt and leather jacket. It was risky, but so was being unarmed.

I went into the saloon bar, and there was a geezer with a beard and a beer gut propping up one end of the counter next to a fruit machine.

I went up and stood about a yard from him, and ordered a lager top from the barmaid. I took out my cigarettes, extracted one from the packet, put it in my mouth and tapped my pockets.

'Got a light, mate?' I said to Beer Gut, and he obliged with a gold Dunhill.

I went over to the CD jukebox and chose a selection of records. First up was Madness. The music was loud in the empty room, but that suited me fine.

I went back and took a mouthful of sweet beer, and I sensed Beer Gut was giving me the once over.

I looked at him and said, 'Poxy night.'

He nodded.

'Drink?' I asked.

'Don't mind if I do. Sam Smith's.'

I caught the barmaid's eye and ordered a pint of bitter for him, and a Scotch for myself.

The first record ended and the second one I'd chosen started. 'My Girl' by the Temptations. I love that song.

'You might be able to help me,' I said.

'How's that?'

'I'm looking for a new hat.'

His eyes narrowed. 'What makes you think you'll get one here? This is a pub.'

'I asked around. A friend told me.'

'What friend?'

'His name's Tony. Don't know the other. He works the markets. Knock-off kids' clothes mainly.'

Beer Gut took a sip of his drink and said, 'Cost ya.'

I took out my cigarettes again and offered him one, which he accepted, then took one for myself. As he leaned over to give me a light I gave him one of the bundles of bank notes. It vanished like smoke in the air conditioning.

He finished his pint with a gargantuan swallow. 'Wait here,' he said, and left the pub.

As the last record I'd selected came on, I bought a box of matches and another pint of lager, this time without the lemonade, pulled up a stool and sat down.

I'd finished my third pint and smoked another four cigarettes, and I was beginning to wonder if I'd been mugged off, before Beer Gut returned.

'The cab outside,' he said.

I went to the door and out into the rain that had thickened to a slate-grey downpour, and saw a black cab parked at the kerb with its 'For Hire' sign switched off. I went to the back door and got inside. In the far corner was a large figure muffled up against the weather.

I sat next to him and the cab pulled away with a jerk. The driver was similarly muffled up, and wore a cap pulled low over his eyes.

'Come here, dear,' said the figure next to me, and I felt his hands all over my body as he frisked me down. 'Sorry,' the figure said, 'but I'd hate for our conversation to be broadcast.'

'I'm not wired,' I said.

'I certainly hope not. You'd be dead if you were.'

I believed he meant it.

The cab's tyres sizzled along the wet streets as the driver took us through the back doubles until I was totally lost. I didn't say a word as we went. When my companion wanted to talk to me, I reckoned that he would. Eventually we pulled up under a railway bridge and the driver switched off the engine.

'You need a new hat, I believe,' said the figure.

'That's right.'

'Any particular style?'

'A revolver. Small.'

'Magnum?'

'Not necessarily. What have you got?'

The figure reached under the seat and brought out a box which he placed on his knee and opened. Then he reached up and switched on the dim courtesy light in the back of the cab.

'I have three here that might suit.'

He put his hand into the box and it emerged holding the dark shape of a gun.

'This is a Charter Arms Bulldog Pug,' he said. '.357 Magnum. Five-shot, two-and-a-half-inch barrel with a hammer shroud. Stainless steel. Nice gun.'

He passed it over. It felt good in my hand, but I wasn't keen on the stainless-steel finish.

'How much?' I asked.

'A monkey. Ammunition extra.'

I handed it back. 'What else?'

In went the hand again, and out came another revolver.

'A Smith & Wesson model 624. Fires S&W .44 ammunition.' He gave it to me.

'Too big,' I said, and passed it back to him.

I saw him shrug. Then he stuck in his thumb and pulled out a plum. He handed me a matt black gun with shiny black rubber grips.

'A Colt Commando,' he said. '.38. A very rare gun. Factory fresh.'

I hefted it in my hand. It fitted perfectly. It was small and stubby with a two-inch barrel. And with the black finish, it was almost invisible in the gloom where we were sitting.

'How much?' I asked.

'Six hundred.'

'Pretty steep.'

'Like I said, a rare gun.'

'Ammunition?'

'A box of fifty shells, a century.'

'Don't mess about,' I said.

'Take it or leave it.'

'It's dear.'

'Overheads,' he replied.

I looked round the interior of the vehicle. 'The cost of cab fares *is* prohibitive these days. Five hundred for the Colt and the ammo.'

I heard him laugh.

'Try again,' he said.

'Six hundred. You give me the shells, and pay for the cab.'

He hesitated. 'Done,' he said, after a minute.

I have been, I thought.

I went through my pockets and gave him six packets of one hundred pounds. He counted each one carefully.

When he was satisfied, he reached into the box and took out a box of fifty .38 special ammunition and gave it to me.

'Put it away, dear,' he said. 'I'm the only person who carries loaded firearms in this car,' and I heard the deadly click as he cocked a pistol he produced from somewhere about his person.

'Be cool,' I said. 'I just want a gun, not a gunfight.' I put the Colt into one pocket of my leather jacket, and the box of bullets into another.

'I'm glad we understand each other,' the figure said, and leaned over and tapped on the partition of the cab with the barrel of his gun.

The driver switched on and pulled away again, and took me back as far as Arding & Hobbs.

'You don't mind if I drop you off here, dear, do you?' asked the figure. 'The pub's just up the road. I'm sure you've got a car near it, and I don't want you to follow me or anything silly like that. If you want to sell the gun back, I'll give you twenty-five per cent of what you paid, anytime. Just see my friend who you saw before. He's in most evenings. It's been a pleasure.'

'Thanks,' I said, and got out of the cab at the lights, and walked back to the Jag in the driving rain.

34

When I got home I checked the action of the gun, and dry fired it a couple of times. It seemed fine, so I loaded it with six brass-jacketed bullets from the box the geezer in the cab had sold me.

Dawn called me at around ten, to tell me that she and Tracey were safe and well at Tracey's mum's in Milton Keynes, and to give me the phone number there. She was adamant that they hadn't been followed. I trusted her judgement. She told me to be careful. I told her the same. I didn't tell her I'd bought a revolver.

I called Jacqueline Harvey at the hotel. She was in her room.

'Hi,' I said. 'It's me. Nick. How was dinner?'

'Wonderful. They've got an excellent chef here. And Toby was great company.'

So it was Toby now.

'I look forward to joining you tomorrow,' I said. 'Unless you've got a heavy date with old Toby, that is.'

I almost felt her blush over the phone.

'Don't be silly,' she said. 'You almost sound jealous.'

'I almost am. He's a lot younger and fitter than me.'

'But you're you.'

'Thanks, Jackie,' I said. 'I appreciate that.'

'It's the truth.'

I changed the subject. 'I'm meeting the news editor from the paper tomorrow at lunchtime; I'll ring you when I get back. OK?'

'I'll expect your call.'

'And I'll see you tomorrow evening.'

'I wish you were here now.'

'Me too,' I said. And I did.

'I'm lonely, Nick.'

'Me too,' I said again. I didn't mention Toby. The time for teasing was over.

'Goodnight,' she said.

'Goodnight, Jackie.'

And I put down the phone.

It was true that I was lonely. But it was Dawn I missed the most. Up until then I hadn't even realised that it was. I'd have to watch that.

The night passed quietly. I slept with the Colt under my pillow, and took it with me when I went for a piss at three a.m.

I called King's the next morning and the ward sister told me that Chas was on the mend, although not talking yet.

That made me feel better.

I took the gun with me when I went to meet Slade.

That made me feel better too.

I was in the Crown & Sceptre by eleven forty-five. It was a big old boozer on a corner, with seats and tables outside on the pavement. *Très* continental, and just right for a lungful of carbon monoxide. I went inside and asked behind the counter for Tom Slade. The barman sent me into the back where a grey-haired geezer in a dodgy sports coat was sitting, with a briefcase and the biggest pile of linens I've ever seen on the table in front of him.

'Tom Slade?' I asked.

'Sharman?'

I nodded agreement, and he pushed the papers to one side, gestured for me to sit down, and asked what I wanted to drink.

'Lager,' I said.

He went to the bar, got me a drink, and brought it back, plus one more for himself.

When we were sitting comfortably, we began.

'Have you seen Chas?' I asked.

Slade nodded.

'Is it true that he can't talk? Or is that hospital flannel?' I asked.

'It's true,' said Slade. 'He's under sedation, and his jaw's wired up. He's not a well boy, but he'll survive.'

'I'm pleased to hear it,' I said. 'And I'm pleased to hear you're still considering using the story.'

'It's a good story,' he said. 'Or it would be if you could supply us with corroborating evidence. Some *hard* corroborating evidence.'

'I will.' I hoped I sounded more convincing than I felt. If there was nothing at Collier's I was well fucked.

'You'd better, or we'll have to drop it.'

'Jackie's sister was murdered. She was abused. Isn't what I wrote down, plus her story, hard enough evidence?'

He gave me a pitying look for my naivety. 'Not in this day and age, son. The libel settlements are getting bigger every week. We can't afford to take a flyer with a story like this. Sorry. It has to have backing.'

I didn't like the 'son' bit. 'I told you, it will,' I said. 'And thanks for taking care of Jackie, whatever happens.'

'No problem.'

'I'd hate for what happened to Chas to happen to her.'

'You think he was given a beating because of the story?' asked Slade.

I gave him a pitying look for his naivety, but stopped short of calling him 'son'. 'Don't you?'

'It's possible.'

'More than that,' I said. 'It's definite. I got a phone call.'

'You didn't tape it by any chance?' This guy was beginning to get right up my nose.

'No. I didn't tape it,' I said.

'And it was the same people who gave you a going over?'

'The same policemen, yes. I didn't know you knew about that.'

'I did.'

'Then you know that, even without so-called hard evidence, someone out there doesn't want this story to go ahead. The only reason can be that we're on the right track.'

'I agree. But even so, *without* corroboration I can't move. And if you're so sure, why come to us? Go straight to the police yourself.'

Another one. When were these people going to rent a room in the real world?

'Police did it,' I said exasperatedly. 'You don't set one copper on to another. For Christ's sake, Slade, where have you been? You work for a Sunday paper. Surely sometime in your career you've come across a bad copper.'

'Yes, I have,' he said. 'You, for one.'

Jesus. So that was it. 'Terrific,' I said. 'They've been to see you, and told you all my family secrets in passing?'

He nodded.

'And?' I asked.

He pulled a face. 'Have they been to see *you*?' he asked.

'Course they have. They may be dumb as shit, but even *they* worked out it was the same people worked me and Chas over. Especially as it was me took him to the hospital. But you haven't answered my question. What did you tell them?'

'Nothing.'

'Thank Christ for that. Nor did I. I played dumb. So tell me, how far had Chas got with the story? Do you at least have a start?'

'Of course. Chas was working from a desk in the office. And I was keeping this in my safe.' He opened his briefcase and took out my exercise book. Boy was I glad to see it. I'd been wondering where the hell it had got to. 'The story's on disc,' Slade went on. 'And we're putting another writer on to it. His name's Walter Sturridge. He's good. A staff man. It'll run next Sunday if you can give me something that the lawyers will go with.'

'The sooner the better,' I said. 'And tell him to be careful. People who get involved in this caper tend to spend an inordinately long time in hospital.'

'He'll be careful. I've put two more of our security staff on to him, twenty-four hours a day.'

'Good. And that was a good idea putting your man into the hotel. I feel better knowing that Jackie isn't on her own,' I said.

He shrugged. 'It's par for the course with a story as sensitive as this one.'

Even if you don't know if you can use it, I thought. You bastard. Keep her well away from the competition just in case.

'I hope they're as good as you say. Tell them to expect the worst. Collier and his pals fight as dirty as shit,' I said.

'They can take care of themselves.'

'I certainly hope so.'

'They're ex-SAS. Just like Toby Gillis.'

'They need to be, believe me.'

'Point taken. Another drink?'

I accepted. He was on exes, I wasn't. In fact I wasn't on anything. Except a possible disability pension. What a mug punter I was turning out to be.

When he came back with another beer for me and Scotch for himself, he said, 'Walter's going through everything that Chas put on to disc. Tomorrow he'll want to talk to Jacqueline Harvey. There won't be any problem will there?'

'Not that I can see. She'd like me to be there, I know that.'

'That's fine,' said Slade. 'Then Walter can talk to you as well.'

I nodded.

Slade sank his Scotch in one and gathered his stuff together. 'I'm off back to the office, then,' he said. 'You'll be at the number you gave me today?'

'Or at the hotel,' I replied. 'Jackie and I are having dinner tonight.'

'Enjoy your meal,' he said, shook my hand and left.

I finished my pint and went back to the car, and home.

35

When I got there, I telephoned the Fortescue and asked for Miss Clancey. I got put straight through.

'Jackie,' I said. 'Nick.'

'Hello. What's happening?'

I told her that I'd seen Slade, and that everything was progressing well. I didn't mention what he'd said about dropping the story if I couldn't come up with some hard evidence.

When I'd finished, I asked, 'How's Toby today?'

'Fine. We had breakfast and lunch together. It's really weird, I feel like Madonna or someone with my own bodyguard.'

'Where is he now?'

'In the next room. He told me I should get some rest. I must admit this is all a bit of a strain. I'm not used to anything like it.'

'You'll be all right,' I assured her. 'Just stay calm.'

'I will. Are you still coming for dinner tonight?'

'Of course. I'll be with you by seven. But I have to split about eleven-thirty. I've got to see a man about a dog.'

'Couldn't you come over a bit earlier then? I'd really like to see you.'

I looked at my watch. It wasn't quite three.

'Sure,' I said. 'I'm not doing anything special.'

'I'd appreciate it.'

'All right. I'll make a call, and I'll come right over.'

'I'll look forward to it,' she said.

We made our farewells, and I rang the number Dawn had given me in Milton Keynes.

Tracey answered. She told me that Dawn was out. I told her that I was going out too, and wouldn't be back until quite late. Then I was going out again. I explained what had been happening and gave her the number of the hotel, just in case. She told me to call when I got home, however late it was. I said that I would. I asked her how they both were. She told me they were fine. She told me that she loved me, and I said that I loved her too, and to send my love to Dawn, and we both hung up. I stood looking at the phone and wondered how it would all end. Then I shrugged and left. When you start wondering things like that you can go crazy.

I drove to Bayswater in the Cavalier, the Colt Commando tucked into the belt of my blue jeans.

The receptionist told me that Miss Clancey was in the lounge taking afternoon tea.

I swanned in and found her and Toby chattering prettily together over the remains of a plate of scones with clotted cream and jam.

'Hello,' I said, as I pulled up a chair to their table. 'Having fun?'

Jacqueline coloured up to match the preserve she was eating, and even Toby seemed a trifle embarrassed. 'I'll leave you two alone,' he said. 'I don't want to intrude.'

'No need,' I replied. 'I talked to Tom Slade today and he told me that you're OK.'

'That was very kind of him,' said Toby.

'But I'll tell you what I told him,' I said. 'Be very careful. The people we're dealing with here play for keeps. This all goes back a very long time, and it's serious. I don't know what Jackie's told you, but keep your mind on business. This is all very nice and cosy, the afternoon tea and all, but it could change in a second, if they find out what's going on here. I know. I got a good beating because of it, and so did the writer I involved.'

'I'll bear that in mind,' said Toby. 'But I didn't get this job because of my charm.'

'So I gather,' I said. 'And believe me, your being here makes me feel a whole lot better. It's just that I don't want anyone else getting hurt. Anyone else on our side that is.'

We were interrupted by the arrival of a waitress who took my order for another pot of tea and some more scones with jam and clotted cream.

Whilst we waited for her to fetch them, I pinched a corner of Jackie's last cake, and we talked inconsequentially about nothing much at all.

When the waitress reappeared, I let her be mother with my tea.

'So how's the hotel?' I asked, around a mouthful of scone.

'It's great,' said Jackie. 'It's like a holiday.' At least her mood seemed to be improving, and I'd bet it had something to do with the presence of Toby on the scene.

'And the chef's good?' I said.

'Really good.'

'Oh, well,' I said. 'At least you can eat free for the next few days. And talking of that, this bloke Walter Sturridge, the writer – he wants an interview with both of us tomorrow. Are you going to be all right with that, Jackie?'

'Will you be there?'

'Of course, if you want me.'

'And Toby?'

'Sure.'

Jackie got up and went to the loo, and I said to Toby, 'I hope your intentions are honourable towards her. It looks like she's starting to rely on you. She's been through some shit in her life, and it's not over yet.'

'Perfectly honourable,' he replied. 'I'm becoming very fond of her. She told me a little of what happened. And anything I can do to help, I will.'

'That's good, Toby,' I said. 'Just don't let her down.'

'I won't. For instance, if I didn't know who you were, you wouldn't have got within five yards of this table carrying what you're carrying on your left side.'

I touched the butt of the gun through my jacket. 'Very good,' I said. 'I didn't realise it was that obvious. Are you carrying?'

'Of course. But mine's legal. I imagine yours isn't.'

'You imagine right. You're not going to shop me, are you?'

He smiled. 'No. I just hope you can use it.'

'I can,' I assured him.

Right then, Jackie came back and sat down again.

'Are you going to join us for dinner tonight?' I asked Toby.

'It's not really part of my brief,' he replied.

'Oh, do,' said Jackie. Then looked at me. 'As long as you don't mind, Nick.'

'Will I be gooseberry?' I asked. 'Or aren't they on the menu?'

'Silly,' she said, and I poured myself another cup of tea.

36

I drove home fast after dinner and phoned Tracey's mother's number straight away. Tracey answered the phone. 'Hello, doll,' I said. 'How's your luck?'

'Not too bad,' she said. 'Me and mum went up the bingo, I was just one number off the full house.'

'That's the story of my life,' I said.

Tracey giggled. 'Do you want to talk to Dawn?' she asked. 'She's here.'

'Yeah,' I replied.

I heard muffled voices, and Dawn came on. 'Hello,' she said.

'Hello, babe. Did you go to the bingo too?'

'No. That's not my style. But Tracey's mum had a good time. So did Trace.'

'I miss you,' I said.

'I miss you too.'

'Are you all right for cash? I could send some up if you're short.'

'No, we're fine.'

'You sure?'

'Sure. How's your friend?'

'Getting better. And Jacqueline Harvey's tucked up safely in a hotel, courtesy of the publisher who's doing the story.'

'Good. Are you taking care of yourself?'

I thought about the Colt that was lying on the pillow next to me, and where I was going in a few minutes.

'I'm trying,' I said.

'Be careful.'

'I will. I take it there's no sign of anyone lurking about where you are.'

'No.'

That was good news, but then there were only so many in Collier's little clique, and they couldn't be everywhere at once, so it looked like Dawn and Tracey had got away clean.

'It's not us you should worry about, Nick, it's you.'

'That's why you're where you are, so I can concentrate on worrying about myself. I'll be all right, Dawn, I promise. Just have a quiet few days up there. The story's going in this Sunday,' I said, crossing my fingers. 'Once it's published we'll all be safe.'

'It's a long time till Sunday,' she said.

'It'll go in a flash. Listen, I'm going to get some sleep. I'm being interviewed tomorrow by the writer who's taken over from Chas. I'll ring you again tomorrow night, OK?'

'I'll look forward to it, Nick; it's lovely to hear your voice.'

'And yours,' I said. 'I really do miss you.'

'You sound surprised.'

'I am a bit.'

'Should I be flattered?'

'I don't know. Probably not.'

'Well I am, a bit.'

'Good. Give my love to Tracey.'

'I will. I love you, Nick.'

'I love you too,' I said. And I meant it.

'Goodnight,' she said, and her voice sounded ghostly down the line, like she was going away from me, and I gripped the phone tighter.

'Goodnight,' I whispered. 'And be careful.'

She didn't say any more, just hung up the phone gently in my ear, and I sat on the side of the bed holding the receiver and staring at the black gun on the white pillowcase beside me, then got set to meet Monkey Mann.

37

I was ready as instructed by half-twelve. I quickly changed into black Levi's, black DMs with nice soft soles, and a black nylon jacket over a navy T-shirt. I did have one thing with me. A portable Canon copier that I'd hired from a shop in Tottenham Court Road. It was not much bigger than a sheet of foolscap paper and wafer thin in its carrying case, the most bulky thing about it being the three-pin plug that was attached to its wire, and the deposit I'd had to leave in the shop.

And the Colt of course. Tucked into my belt, just in case.

I peered though the curtains of my darkened room until the sleek shape of a new Ford Granada saloon appeared beneath me and flashed its headlights once. I went downstairs and out into the street, walked over to the Ford and saw Monkey's face grinning through the driver's window. I went round to the passenger side and got in. The courtesy light didn't come on. 'Nice wheels,' I said.

'Comfortable,' he agreed. 'The bloke who bought this's got taste. Full option pack fitted.' The Granada slid away and turned in the direction of Peckham.

We said little on the journey until Monkey expertly manoeuvred the car into a space about two hundred yards away from Collier's house with a clear view of his front door between the parked cars that crowded both kerbs. I could see a dim light through the bull's-eye glass. The street was deserted and peaceful.

'Nice of him to leave a bit of illumination,' remarked Monkey as he leaned into the back of the car and took out a leather satchel. 'I'll be back in half a mo. Keep your head down.'

I did as instructed. He left the car and snaked along the pavement, almost invisible in the dark clothes he was wearing.

I waited for five, then ten minutes, and was just starting to get worried when the driver's door opened again and Monkey slid in beside me.

'So?' I said.

'Patience,' he replied, and reached into the satchel and removed a plastic gizmo that looked like the remote control for a TV set. A tiny red light fluttered against the matt black plastic of the device.

'Ready?' he said.

I nodded and Monkey touched a pad on the gizmo. The red light winked out and Collier's alarm came into life. The full Monty. Twin bells, and the blue light on top of the alarm box began to flash. The sound was very loud even where we were, tightly enclosed in the car, and must have been deafening close up.

'A little damp in the control box. That's the weak spot in the system, where the electrical supply from outside and the phone lines connect,' explained Monkey. 'It often happens.'

'How?'

'I did a Jimmy in it. I told you it was a piece of piss. And fitted a little invention of my own. Don't worry. It looks like it's part of the works if anyone takes a gander. And by the time Telecom gets to it, it'll be gone.'

'Nice. What happens now?'

'The cops'll be here soon. They always look after their own.'

'And?'

'You'll see. Relax.'

We both did, adjusting the seats so that we weren't visible from outside but could just see Collier's place from over the dashboard. First of all a few lights came on in the neighbouring houses, and one or two people peered through their curtains. Then some of the braver souls came out into the street and stood together outside Collier's front gate and one was even daring enough to take a look over the back gate. Within ten minutes, just like Monkey had predicted, a crime car and a police Mini-Metro arrived on the scene to add more blue lights to the one winking over Collier's front door. The Old Bill had a word with the neighbours then wandered round the back themselves.

'The alarm should only ring for twenty minutes,' said Monkey. 'That's the new law. But sometimes the circuit gets well fucked and it starts again.'

Once again his prediction was right. Twenty minutes exactly after he pressed the button on his remote control, the alarm died, leaving just an echo in my ears, and the tiny red light on the remote sparked into life again.

'Give it a minute,' said Monkey, as the coppers all congregated in the tiny front garden again.

He allowed fifty seconds to pass before hitting the pressure pad again, and the alarm started once more, sounding even louder if that were possible.

'I hope your man's about,' said Monkey. 'We need the keys now.'

Ten minutes more passed before Collier's Sierra sped round the corner, skidded to a halt behind the police cars, and he jumped out and joined his colleagues in front of his house. Even from two hundred yards away I could almost see the steam coming out of his ears. He let himself in the house and a few seconds later the alarm stopped again, and the light on the remote came on.

'Now the fun really begins,' said Monkey. 'He'll reset the alarm and hope it works OK. But of course we know better.' After maybe half a minute, Collier came out of the house and slammed the door behind him, then stood with an ear cocked before saying something to the coppers.

'Seems like a shame to disappoint him,' said Monkey and touched the pad for a third time, and the alarm started again.

Collier threw up his arms in exasperation. He went into the house and once again the alarm stopped.

'Do you think he'll try once more or give up?' asked Monkey.

It appeared to be the latter, as Collier reappeared just a second or two later, slammed the door, turned the mortise lock and shrugged at the uniforms.

'And that should be that for a bit,' said Monkey. 'A loose connection in the wiring and everyone goes about their business.'

'What about Telecom?' I asked as Collier and the uniforms got into their cars and drove away, the few lights that had been switched on in the neighbouring houses were turned out again, and the street became peaceful once more.

'They won't be about for hours. Your pal's got to phone them first. And it's late. Besides he's earning his living. He doesn't want to hang around waiting for them when he could be out nicking poor innocent villains. And even if he did phone, and they did come round for a look, they can't get in. Which is where we'll be. They'll just take a shufti at the junction box. No, Mr S. Don't worry. They won't get here till morning and we'll be long gone by then. Coming?' He opened the door of the car and, carrying the satchel, set off in the direction of Collier's place.

I was right behind him, the copier bumping against the gun on my hip, and we climbed over the back gate into the tiny walled garden. Monkey opened an electrical conduit with a minuscule electric screwdriver and removed something which he dropped into his pocket before replacing the cover. 'Not even a scratch on the screws,' he whispered. 'Now let's get inside.'

He slid on a pair of surgeon's rubber gloves which he removed from his satchel, and gave me a pair which I pulled over my hands. There were two locks on the back door: a Yale and a mortise. He picked the mortise and loided the Yale. We were inside within a minute and a half of him reaching the door. He stood inside the kitchen and sniffed the still air. 'Now where's this safe?' he said to himself. 'Come out wherever you are, you little devil.'

He produced a torch from his bag and switched it on. It gave just a needle point of light and I guessed that it wouldn't be noticed from outside. I followed him through the house as he peered behind pictures and under carpets.

The safe was set in concrete, in the airing cupboard next to the bathroom, behind the towels.

'Sweet,' he said, and carefully placed the clean laundry on the carpet and got to work on the combination lock, his torch clenched between his teeth. He had some other electronic device with him, which he attached to the face of the safe next to the lock. As he moved the dial, a digital read-out on the face of the device blinked redly. After about five minutes Monkey chuckled around the torch, took it out of his mouth, pulled open the safe door and stepped aside. 'Jap crap,' he said disgustedly. 'My kid could open it with a spoon.'

I took the torch from him and peered inside the safe. There was cash in there. A lot of cash. All neatly banded. Enough to make Monkey's eyes glisten, and some jewellery, and at the back a wallet full of papers. I ignored the dough and the tom and pulled out the wallet.

'There's no window in the bathroom,' said Monkey. 'We can put the light on in there.'

He was right. We went inside, closed the door and put on the light. After allowing a minute for my eyes to adjust I sat on the closed toilet seat and opened the wallet. Monkey perched on the edge of the bathtub.

Inside the wallet was the usual: passport; life insurance; insurance papers for the building and contents; old photos; Collier's birth certificate. And the not so usual: the deeds for the house we were in – no mortgage, unusual for a copper. Plus the deeds and blueprints for a house in Marbella. A big one with five bedrooms, a pool and a private slice of sea front. Very tasty – and expensive. And a paying-in book for a deposit account in an American bank, the Jersey branch – no nasty British Inland Revenue snoopers there. The total of the investments almost brought tears to my eyes too. That, the cash in the safe, and the house in Marbella all added up to a nice little retirement for Collier. And finally, at the back of the wallet, I found what I was looking for. A plain white envelope, just slightly yellow with age. Inside the envelope was Byrne's signed confession to the rape and murder of Carol Harvey. A single handwritten sheet, signed and dated, folded twice, that spelled it all out. Sweet as. Collier, I've got you, you slimebag, I thought.

'Is that what you're looking for?' asked Monkey.

'Yeah.'

'Good. What now?'

'I make a copy of it, and we put everything back exactly where it was and split.'

'Fair enough.'

We left the bathroom, turning off the light as we went. In the hall was an electrical socket. I took the copier out of its case, plugged it in and switched it on. I opened the top and placed the confession inside, face down, then pressed the 'Copy' button. There was a whirr from inside, and a neatly printed sheet of A4 paper slid out from a slot in the top of the machine. I looked at it in the light from Monkey's torch and it seemed OK, but took a second copy for luck. Then I refolded the original into its deep creases and returned it to its envelope, and the envelope to the wallet next to the other papers.

Then we put everything back as we had found it and left the house by the back door again, Monkey locking it as we went. We scrambled over the gate and back to the car. Monkey drove carefully away, not putting on the lights until we were in the next street. By two in the morning we were back at my place. I paid Monkey the balance of his grand, and he drove off back to Beckenham.

And that was that.

38

I could hardly sleep when I got in, and was up by seven-thirty. I phoned Tom Slade at his office at eight. He was in. Maybe he hadn't been able to sleep either.

'I was just going to call you,' he said.

'Why?'

'Can you be at the hotel at midday?' he said.

'If I can see you before.'

'Why?'

'I've got it.'

'What?'

'The hard proof you need to go with the story big time.'

'*What?*'

'You heard,' I said triumphantly. At last in this case I had reason.

'What is it?'

'A confession. Written on the day that Carol Harvey died, and signed by Alan Byrne.'

'I don't believe it. A confession to murder. Where did you get it?'

'Believe it. But I'd rather not say where I got it if you don't mind.'

'Can I see it?'

'That's why I phoned.'

'Can you come over straight away?'

'Of course.'

'You know where we are?'

'I do.'

'How long will it take you to get here?'

'Depends on the traffic. Give me three quarters of an hour.'

'Ask for me at security. They'll pass you straight through.'

'OK,' I said and hung up.

I took one copy of the confession with me and left the other in the hiding place I'd made under the eaves of the house, then I tucked the Colt into the pocket of my leather jacket and went out to my car. It took me exactly forty minutes to make the journey. When I arrived at the newspaper offices it was more like going into Stalag Luft IV. Barbed wire on the gates. The whole bit. Talk about Fortress Wapping. But I was expected and got directed to the car park. A woman came out of a door in the nearest building and over to the car. 'Nick Sharman?' she said.

'That's right.'

'Come this way. Tom's waiting for you.'

And he was. In a comfortable office awash with papers and with a view of the river.

He stood up as I entered and shook my hand. When I was seated and coffee had been served, he said, 'Can I see it?'

I took the copy of Byrne's confession from my pocket, unfolded it and passed it to him. He took a long time reading the few lines, then looked up at me. 'A copy,' he said. 'Where's the original?'

'Where I left it.'

'And that is?'

'I told you, I'd rather not say.'

'I must insist I'm afraid.'

I hesitated. But what was the point of keeping it secret?

'Fair enough. In a safe in Detective Inspector Terry Collier's dream house in Peckham. But not the dream house he plans to move to when he retires, if I'm any guesser.'

'And where would that be?'

'Marbella.'

'Very nice.'

'But you know what they say?'

'What?'

'In every dream house, a heartache. And I plan to be the heartache for our friend Collier. The slimy little cocksucker.'

'You don't like him much, do you?'

'You're very perceptive.' Christ, the cunt had beaten me nearly to death. What was I supposed to do? Put him on top of my Christmas card list?

'And how did you get the copy?' asked Slade.

'How do you think? I broke into his house and did the peter. Simple.'

'Against the law.'

This guy seemed determined to rain on my parade.

'In this case, most of the law seems to be on the wrong side. Now, do you believe what Jackie and I have been saying or not?'

'How do I know this is Byrne's handwriting and signature?'

'Jesus, Slade. He was Assistant Commissioner in the Met. The handwriting on that note is pretty distinctive. Check it out. He might even have written to this paper at some time. You know, after one of your crusades against litter louts or video nasties, or something really wicked like that.'

Slade didn't rise to my bait.

'You could be right,' he agreed. 'Can you leave this with me?'

I nodded.

'Of course you realise,' he said, 'if this confession is genuine, you could just take it to the police yourself.'

I smiled grimly. I still didn't trust Old Bill. Not completely. And doing that would spoil the fun of all the naughty boys reading about themselves over coffee and croissants on a bright Sunday morning. 'I want the maximum publicity,' I said. 'Let's just leave it as it is, shall we?'

'We may have to take the file to the police ourselves in any case,' he said. 'In fact it's almost definite that we shall. The probability is that we'll print the story without naming names, and let the police pull them in. Then our daily sister paper will take up the story.'

'But you won't deliver the goods to the police before the paper comes out, will you?'

He shook his head.

'That's OK. I don't care what happens then. In fact I know just the copper to show this little lot to. He's a scruffy git, based at Gipsy Hill nick. Name of Robber.'

'Unfortunate name,' said Slade. 'For a policeman.'

'Unfortunate or not, he's straight,' I said. 'He won't take any nonsense from them. Not when he's given proof like this. But I don't want him sticking his oar in until the paper's on the streets.'

Slade nodded. 'And you'll go to the hotel this morning?'

I nodded back.

'Right. Walter Sturridge is going to interview Jacqueline Harvey. I've already talked to Toby, and he's going to brief her this morning. After Walter's spoken to her, he wants to talk to you. I expect it'll take the best part of the day.'

'Suits me,' I said.

'I'll have this checked out this morning.' He tapped the piece of paper in front of him. 'I'll talk to you later at Fortescue's. OK?'

I nodded for a third time, then said, 'How's Chas?'

'Getting better apparently.'

'I'm going to drop in at the hospital on the way to the hotel. I don't know if they'll let me see him, but at least he'll know I've been.'

'If you do speak to him, give him my best,' said Slade. 'And if there's anything he needs, just let me know.'

'OK,' I said. 'I'll talk to you soon.'

'You will.'

He showed me back to the car park and I drove to King's College Hospital.

Chas was asleep when I got there, but they let me poke my head into the private room the paper was paying for, and I left a note for him on the pad next to his bed.

He looked very pale and drawn lying there with his jaw wired shut.

At the end of the note I told him I'd be dropping in sometime over the next couple of days, and I'd tell him all the latest hot dish, and that things were going well.

I spoke to the sister who looked after him, and she said he was doing as well, if not better, than expected. Physically that is. Mentally there was no way of knowing what kind of scars a beating like that would leave.

By the time I got back into the car I was angry again. As angry as when it was me who'd been given a going-over. I touched the heavy weight of the gun in my pocket for reassurance, and drove to the Fortescue.

I was there by eleven, and found Jackie and Toby in the lounge having coffee. She was ashen and I knew that the thought of telling a stranger what she'd told me about the abuse she'd suffered as a child, and what had happened to her sister, and the estrangement from her father, was taking its toll.

I ordered a fresh pot of coffee from the waiter, then told them what I'd found at Collier's house. If I expected Jackie to turn cartwheels, I was disappointed, but at least Toby Gillis seemed to cheer up at the news.

'Nick,' she said, seeing how I looked at her lack of enthusiasm, 'I'm sorry. You've done a great job. You've been so brave, and looked after me so well. But it's just talking to this reporter. I'm dreading it. Going over everything again. I don't know if I can cope.'

I went over to her, crouched down beside the chair that she was sitting in, and held her hand.

'Of course you'll be able to cope,' I said. 'Listen, Jackie, I know this is going to be hard on you, but Toby and I will be there. What happened to you and Carol is nothing to be ashamed of. It wasn't your fault. Always remember that. I know the bastard who did it to you tried to make you think that it was. That's how they operate. That's why they get away with it. I saw it often enough when I was in the job. Men like that count on it. They prey on kids because they can't handle real grown-up people. No matter how tough they look, inside they're frightened little rabbits. You've got to hold on to that thought. You're stronger than he'll ever be. I know that. I knew it the minute you told me what had happened. That took courage. I admire you for it. But if you can't talk about it, you can't. Nobody's going to blame you.'

'I would,' she said.

'I know, and that's why I know you're going through with it, horrible as it is.'

'I just feel so strange. Everyone's going to know.'

'I know.'

'I haven't got many friends, but the people at work...' She didn't finish.

'Jackie,' I said. 'Believe me, you've got friends. There's the two of us here for a start.'

Toby smiled at her reassuringly.

Jackie tried a weak smile of her own in return. 'I know,' she said again.

I squeezed her hand tighter. 'And it's the truth,' I said. 'With the confession I found, it'll all be over with by Monday.'

Even that didn't seem to make her feel much better.

'And I spoke to Slade this morning,' I went on. 'In the first instance the paper probably won't even name names. Then as soon as the first edition is out, they'll pass everything we know on to the police. The whole file. They won't be able to ignore it then. Not with the publicity the story will generate. Collier, Millar, Grisham and your uncle will be nicked by Sunday morning, and we'll all be safe. Safe forever.'

Kind of a rash promise, I thought, even as I said it. But before Jackie could say anything back, the waiter came over with the coffee and saved me.

'Three large cognacs,' I said to him.

Toby shook his head, and the waiter gave me a quizzical look, like they do.

'Bring 'em anyway,' I said. 'I think we'll need them before this morning's over.'

Walter Sturridge was very punctual. He came into the lounge at twelve noon precisely. He was in his early thirties I imagined, short, blond, with a bald patch surrounded by curly hair that looked like it might fly away in a strong breeze. He was wearing a grunge-green suit, possibly an Armani that had been through a rough time, over a cream shirt and a tie patterned with green foliage, untidily knotted to show where the top button of his shirt was fastened. His shoes were brown suede with the toes scuffed out, and the unfortunate suit's pockets bulged with pens, papers, a couple of notebooks, a portable phone, a tape recorder, and a packet of cassette tapes. His face was round with pale skin and rosy cheeks. He stopped at the door, looked round, and immediately came over in our direction.

'Toby,' he said to Gillis.

Toby nodded.

'And you must be Jacqueline Harvey,' said Sturridge, and stuck out his hand in Jackie's direction. She took it, and he gave hers a sharp shake.

'And you're Sharman,' he said finally, letting his pale blue eyes focus on me.

I nodded.

'I've written about you before. You *do* manage to get into some scrapes.'

'I was born under a bad sign,' I said.

'You can say that again,' he replied, and leant over and offered his mitten to me. I took it, and got another short, sharp shake for my troubles.

Sturridge pulled up a chair and said, 'Jacqueline, I want to talk to you first. There's a conference room upstairs that I've booked for the entire day. Lunch can be served there, or we can come back downstairs, depending on your preference. I understand you want Toby and Mr Sharman present for the interview. Is that right?'

Jackie nodded.

'Fine. When we've finished I intend to get Mr Sharman's –'

'Call me Nick,' I interrupted.

He deferred to me with a nod. 'Nick's side of things. And please call me Walter. Not Wally, if you don't mind. I hope to have it all wrapped up by dinner time. If not, or if there's anything further, I trust I can see you again.'

Jackie nodded once more.

Sturridge turned to me. 'I understand you've been busy, Nick,' he said, and took a sheet of paper out of the inside pocket of his jacket. 'Tom Slade faxed this over to me before I left home.' He placed the paper face up on the table next to the cups. It was a copy of Byrne's confession.

'Before I saw this, I must admit I was doubtful. I've read what Chas Singleton put down on disc, and I know what happened to him, and to you, Nick. And I've read what you wrote in your journal of events. I've checked up also on Grant's suicide. And gone back further and looked into what happened to Carol Harvey in Brixton all that time ago, and Grant's subsequent confession and conviction. It all fitted together nicely with what you've told us, except for one thing.'

'What?' I said.

'There was absolutely no proof that the police officers concerned did what you two say they did.' He looked at Jackie. 'And weren't, in fact, just doing their jobs properly, when they arrested Grant for the rape and murder of your sister.' Under his gaze, she paled, then blushed red.

'Forgive me,' he said. 'I don't mean to upset you. But you must admit I had a point. And as for your uncle. Well, he *did* end up as Assistant Commissioner of the Metropolitan Police, and retired without a blemish on his character. But now, with this' – he pointed at the paper – 'we're going to have the bastard. Well and truly. And I'm going to enjoy seeing him squirm when we publish on Sunday.'

39

Sturridge was a very professional interviewer. But then I suppose working for the paper he worked for, he'd need to be. He interrogated Jackie for four hours, with a break for lunch around two. I could tell she hated telling him what had happened between her uncle and her sister and herself. Toby sat close by her, and after a little while kept a firm hold on her hand. I sat in the corner and chain-smoked. Sometimes I could tell that the words she spoke were so painful for her that I wanted to call a halt on the whole thing, but somehow I couldn't.

At three, Slade called and spoke to Sturridge. He didn't say much, just listened, then passed the phone to me.

'The handwriting checks out,' said Slade. 'Good work. Sunday it is.'

'Thank Christ,' I said.

'I'll keep in touch,' he said, and hung up.

When I put down the phone I could see by the look on Jackie's face that Sturridge had told her. I said nothing. Just went back to my seat and lit another cigarette.

By the time the interview was concluded, which was exactly five forty-six by my Rolex, Jackie looked as washed out as my Levi's, and Sturridge had filled a stack of Maxell tapes with her memoirs.

Before Toby took her down to her room, and Sturridge started on me, she came over and took my hand. I stood up.

'Was I all right?' she asked.

'You were great.'

'I've got to go and rest now. Do you need to see me again tonight?'
I shook my head.

'Then I'll see you soon.'

'Whenever you want.'

'Goodnight then.'

'Goodnight… And, Jackie.'

'What?'

'Don't you want to see what your uncle wrote?'

She blanched, and I think she would have fallen if I hadn't grabbed her. I felt like a berk for asking.

'No,' she said. 'I don't. I never want to see it.'

'Fine,' I said. 'Sorry I asked.'

She shook her head, and Toby took her arm and led her out of the room.

Sturridge came over and said, 'Is she all right?'

'She will be,' I replied.

He fitted a new tape into the machine, and started asking me questions. All of a sudden I knew how Jackie had felt.

I told him the story, just like it had happened. Just like I'd written it down in the exercise book that Dawn had bought for me. I left nothing out, and added nothing. As I talked I could feel the sweat soaking through my clothes.

We finished just after eight. I had a terrible headache and a matching thirst, and I wanted to talk to Dawn.

He gathered all his stuff together and stood up.

'Would you like a drink?' he asked.

'Sure.'

We went down to the bar together and he bought me a couple of beers. Then he told me he had to get home and put the interviews down on disc. I didn't press him to stay. I wasn't in the mood for company. After he went I had another beer, then went out into the cold evening air and wandered from bar to bar until chucking-out time. I had two dozen drinks and didn't taste one. Isn't that always the way?

40

The next day and the first part of Friday passed pretty quietly. I spoke to Dawn and Tracey on the phone a couple of times. They said that they were doing fine, but beginning to pine for London. I told them not to bother. They weren't missing much. I spoke to Jackie too, but didn't go and see her. I thought the scars had been reopened deeply enough and were still too raw for that. She said that Toby was taking care of her, and I told her that I was glad.

Otherwise I just sat in the flat, looking at the Colt Commando, and wondering if I'd get a chance to use it on someone, and picking at my guilt like a particularly unattractive scab.

Slade called me on Friday at noon.

'I need a chat,' he said.

'About?'

'I'll tell you when I see you. Can you manage this afternoon?'

'Sure,' I said. 'Where and when?'

'I've got to meet the wife in town later. We're going to the bloody theatre, and I'm taking her out to dinner first, so I'm going for a quick one in Gerry's. Do you know it?'

'Gerry's in Dean Street?'

'Yes.'

Course I knew it. Everybody knows it. Even cabbies know it. It's a subterranean, members-only place where a lot of serious drinking takes place.

'I know it,' I said.

'Four o'clock.'

'I'll be there.'

I took a taxi. I wasn't going to drive. The parking is murder round Shaftesbury Avenue, and there's been lots of times I've gone into Gerry's at lunchtime and come out twelve hours later wondering where I'd left my head.

Before leaving, I tucked the Colt into the pocket of my leather jacket.

The cab got caught in the traffic by Cambridge Circus, and I sat and gazed out of the window at the passers-by. I love Soho. Always have done, always will, no matter what the tourists, and the developers, and the landlords, and the people who used to call themselves yuppies have done to the place. But even they couldn't kill it, hard as they tried. Soho's like mercury. Grind it down under the pad of your thumb, and it'll find its natural level and trickle out from under the side and pop up all bright and silvery. And most of all, I love drinking there in the afternoon, with people who never seem to have a steady job, and the wedge fluctuates from grands one week to shillings the next, and I've seen people counting out piles of pennies for the next Scotch. 'A large one, dear. Mustn't let standards slip.'

I jumped out of the cab and paid it off, then walked down Shaftesbury Avenue towards Dean Street. The door to Gerry's was on the latch, and I pulled it open and went down the stairs into the aquamarine-blue twilight of the bar. There were one or two people sat up at the jump on stools, who looked round as I went down, but no one I knew. Tom Slade was sitting at the table next to the coffee machine. In front of him was a glass half full of beer.

I walked over and he looked up. 'Afternoon,' he said.

I nodded at the glass. 'Another?'

'Beck's.'

I went up to the bar, and smiled at the barmaid, which wasn't hard, the way she looked. 'Good afternoon, Nick,' she said.

'Hello, doll,' I replied. 'Two Beck's please. And one for yourself.'

'Thanks,' she said. 'I don't mind if I do.' She went to the fridge and pulled out two beers and a coke, and I paid for them, took the two bottles of beer and one glass, and went to join Slade at his table.

'So what's up?' I said, when I was sat down with my beer poured out in front of me and a Silk Cut lit.

'We've got a small problem.'

Straight away the alarm bells started ringing.

'What kind of small problem?'

'Don't worry. It's just that Walter spoke to all the police officers involved that he could reach this morning, and we've been threatened with an injunction.'

'He *what*?'

'He spoke to all the officers concerned. All that were available.'

'Christ. You never told me... I thought you weren't going to name names.'

'We're not. Not in the first instance. But it's routine. It'll make an interesting sidebar in the later editions, and next week.'

I could have hit him. 'A fucking sidebar,' I said. My life and Jackie's as a fucking sidebar. 'Are you kidding? He spoke to all of them?'

Slade nodded. 'Almost.'

My heart sank, and I was glad I'd brought the gun with me. From now on, we were in the free-fire zone I'd dreaded. 'What did they say?' I asked.

'Not a lot.'

'Ex-Assistant Commissioner Byrne?'

'No comment. But Walter thought he sounded like he was going to shit himself. Then we had his lawyer on the phone. Threatening us with the injunction I told you about. Don't worry. We're still going to print. Our lawyers are very happy with the story.'

'That's not what I'm worried about, believe me. What about Collier?'

'He told him to fuck off apparently.'

At any other time I would have laughed, but this was no laughing matter. 'Did Sturridge mention the confession, do you know?'

'I don't think he had a chance. But he did to Byrne.'

Which meant they all knew. And the original was probably ashes by now.

'Millar?'

'Put the phone down on him.'

'Grisham?'

'Couldn't contact him. He was out on a case. Like I said, they weren't all available.'

'Did he try Jackie's father?'

'He wasn't around either. He's away until tomorrow on leave. Couldn't be reached.'

Probably just as well, I thought, and I wished for the millionth time that Grant hadn't phoned me, and I hadn't seen him in that pub in Deptford. But what was the point? I couldn't change what had happened, no matter how much I wished. What was it that my old nan used to say to me when I was a kid and wished for something I'd never get? 'If wishes were horses, then beggars would ride.' So true.

'Stupid,' I said, half to myself. 'If they'd just done nothing…'

'What?'

'Forget it. Does Jackie Harvey know that they know?'

'Not from me she doesn't.'

I drank some beer and lit another cigarette.

'I suppose I'd better tell her then.'

'I suppose you'd better. You can phone her from here.'

'I'd rather tell her in person,' I said. 'I'll go over to the hotel and tell her what's happened.'

'How is she?' asked Slade.

'All right, I think. I haven't seen her since the other day, when old Walter dug around in her psyche for four hours. Just spoken to her on the phone. She sounded as well as can be expected. Under the circumstances.'

'Listen, Sharman,' said Slade. 'That's the way it goes. We have to ask the questions to get the answers to build a story. I'm sorry if your friend, or you for that matter, didn't like the way we did it. But that's the way it's done.'

'I understand,' I said wearily, and finished my beer. 'I'd better be off. Enjoy the play.'

And with that, I got up and left the bar.

41

I grabbed a black cab right outside the club and headed for Bayswater. I trolled through the main door and up to the desk and asked for Miss Clancey. The receptionist informed me that she had left the building with two gentlemen, at about four. Just as I'd been meeting Slade at Gerry's.

'Which gentlemen?' I asked, feeling a cold chill creep down my spine.

'I'm sorry,' she said. 'I don't know.'

'Was she with Mr Gillis?'

She shook her head. At least she knew who I was talking about.

'Were the gentlemen from the newspaper?' I asked.

'I don't know,' she said again.

'Was one of them a Mr Sturridge?' I pressed.

She told me she wasn't able to help.

'Did she say when she'd be back?' I asked.

'She didn't leave any message,' said the receptionist.

I asked her to describe the men that Jacqueline had left with. She was pretty vague. But the descriptions she gave could have fitted Collier and Millar. On the other hand they could have fitted ten thousand other adult males in the Greater London area. If not more.

'Is Mr Gillis in?' I asked.

She tried his number, but it didn't answer.

The cold chills were getting worse all the time.

I checked the bars and restaurant, then went back and asked if I could look round Jackie's room. The receptionist wasn't keen. I told her to get the manager. When he arrived, he wasn't keen either, so I gritted my teeth and asked if I could use the phone on the desk. The manager ummed and ahhed, until I wanted to wrap his neck in the phone cord and pull it tight. But eventually he agreed. I looked up the number of Gerry's in my address book, and called the club. Luckily Slade was still there. When he came on the line I told him what was happening. He asked to speak to the manager. I handed the phone over. I don't think the manager got in three words. When he put down the receiver, he gave me a dirty look, and we went upstairs in the lift. Using a passkey he let me in to Jackie's room, and he stood inside the doorway as I took a squint.

Her handbag was still there. The bed was neatly made, a tray of tea things sat on the table, and the TV set was on, tuned into an early-evening soap, with the sound turned down.

There was no sign of a struggle or anything like that.

I opened the bathroom door. It was empty.

'Satisfied?' asked the manager.

'No,' I said.

He tossed his keys in his hand to show displeasure.

'Toby Gillis,' I said. 'In the room next door.'

I thought he was going to give me a blank, but the memory of the phone call from Slade still lingered, and with a sigh we went along the corridor and he threw Toby Gillis's room door open.

The place was in a right two-and-eight: furniture upset, a curtain torn from its runner, and clothes strewn everywhere. There was no sign of Toby. I opened the bathroom door and there he was, dressed in a shirt, slacks and socks, trussed up in the bath with the cord from the shower curtain. Someone had stuffed a flannel into his mouth as a gag. He was rolling about trying to get free, his face was badly bruised, and there was blood in his long blond hair.

Ex-SAS, I thought. God give me strength.

I went over and pulled him out of the tub, and tugged at the knots on his wrists until he was free.

He ripped the gag out of his mouth and said, 'Where's Jackie?'

'You tell me,' I said. 'She left with two men. What happened?'

'One of them knocked at the door and said he was from room service.'

'And you were too busy being charming to check them out. Shit, Toby, what the fuck were you thinking about?'

His face reddened under the bruises.

The manager was standing in the doorway of the bathroom, hopping from one foot to the other.

'Yes?' I said.

'What exactly has been going on here?' he demanded.

'Mind your own business,' I said. 'And get out.'

'This establishment is my responsibility, and if some criminal activity has taken place here, I need to know.'

'Do leave me alone,' I said.

'I insist. I should call the police. And who's going to pay for any damage? I'm sorry, but I may have to ask you to check out.'

'I'm not checked in,' I said. 'And you know damn well who'll pay for the damage. The same people who are paying for the rooms. And if you want to upset them by calling the police, go ahead. But whatever you're going to do, do it now, and leave us alone.'

'I want you out,' he said.

'We're going – in a minute. Now hop it,' I said. 'I need to talk to Mr Gillis.'

For a moment I thought he was going to argue, but he clocked my expression, and he left us to it, closing the door behind him just a little harder than was necessary.

Petulant boy.

I took out my cigarettes and lit one, and looked at Toby.

'Are you all right?' I asked.

'I'll survive.'

'You should have your head examined,' I said.

In more ways than one, I thought, but I didn't say it. He was having a rough enough time as it was. Why make it worse?

'I'll be OK.'

'Suit yourself. Tell me about the geezers who took Jackie.'

His description was better than the receptionist's had been. It had definitely been Collier and Millar. Now, how the fuck had they known where she'd be?

'It was Collier, wasn't it?' said Toby.

'And his sidekick.'

'They're taking some chances aren't they?'

'It's desperation time.' I told him about my conversation with Slade.

'What do we do?'

I took the Colt out of my pocket and weighed it in my hand. 'Leave it to me,' I said. 'I'll sort it. Have you got a motor?'

'Of course.'

'I'm taking it,' I said. 'Give me the keys.'

'I'm coming with you.'

'You should be in the hospital getting your head looked at.'

'I'm coming,' he said again.

I shrugged. 'Come on then,' I said.

'Give me two minutes. I'll meet you in the lobby.'

'Don't be all day about it.'

'I won't.'

I shrugged again and went downstairs. Toby was as good as his word. He joined me a few minutes later wearing a leather jacket over his shirt and trousers, and he'd put on a pair of shoes. His hair was damp where he'd washed the blood out of it.

He took me round to the hotel parking garage where he opened up a black Mercedes 190E.

'Peckham,' I said. 'Do you know it?'

He nodded.

'Let's go then. I'll direct you when we get there.'

He drove well and fast and, despite the heavy Friday-night traffic, we were in Peckham in less than thirty minutes. I told him how to get to Collier's gaff. It was the only place I could think to go. Of course it was deserted. We sat outside in the car, whilst I racked my brains what to do next.

42

I used the car phone in the Mercedes and called Slade on his portable. Toby gave me the number. He'd cancelled his theatre date and was on his way back to his office in a cab. He was well up to speed on developments, having called the hotel back from Gerry's and spoken to the manager.

'Hope I haven't spoiled your evening,' I said drily.

'Listen, Sharman. I didn't want this to happen.'

'Which is why you got Walter Sturridge to make all those calls without bothering to tell either me or Toby.'

'I'm sorry.'

'I hope you don't get sorrier.'

'So do I, believe me.'

It didn't matter if I did or didn't, but I couldn't be bothered to tell him; just said I'd ring him later at the paper, and cut him off.

Then I called Peckham nick. When I got through to the station I asked for either Collier and Millar. Both were off duty. Nothing was known of their whereabouts. Nothing that the bored voice of the female in CID would tell me anyway.

Next I called Millar's home. His wife answered. As far as she was concerned he was out on obbo somewhere. She couldn't or wouldn't enlighten me further. I didn't blame her.

I got through to New Scotland Yard and chased Grisham round

the building for five minutes or so with no luck. I didn't say who I was. He was unavailable. I didn't bother calling Byrne, and Harvey was still on leave.

After that I phoned the paper and spoke to Slade. Just before he'd arrived back at Wapping there'd been an anonymous call to say that if the story ran in the paper on Sunday, then Jacqueline Harvey was going to suffer. Badly. Terminally.

'What did they say to that?' I asked.

'What could they say? No story's worth someone getting hurt.'

'Blimey,' I said. 'Your paper's come over public spirited all of a sudden. What happened? Have you dug up the dirt on some cabinet minister's secret sex life that'll make a better front-page story this week?'

'That's a very cynical outlook,' he said.

'Spare me all that old bollocks,' I replied. 'I'm a victim of the current climate. If that makes me a cynic, then so be it. Who's been told about the call?'

'No one. Like I said, it only came in a few minutes ago. I've been trying to reach you ever since. Where are you?'

'Out and about. On the mean streets. Looking for Jacqueline.'

'I'm sorry, Sharman,' Slade said. 'I really am, whatever you think. I'd just like to know how they knew where Jacqueline Harvey was.'

'Who knows? Maybe someone on your little firm is picking up a few extra readies, leaking out information to interested parties. Maybe she told someone at work where she was, and Collier got it out of them. He can be very persuasive when he wants. He doesn't have to use his fists all the time. He's got a warrant card and that opens a lot of doors. I know. I used to have one myself.'

Slade was silent for a moment. 'Where's Toby?' he asked eventually. 'I heard he got hurt.'

'He's with me.'

Toby glanced in my direction and shook his head.

'Is he all right?' asked Slade.

'As well as can be expected.'

'Let me speak to him.'

I held out the phone and Toby shook his head again.

'I don't think he's interested in speaking to you,' I said to Slade.

'You'd both better come in to the office where we can talk,' he said.

'Not tonight, Josephine,' I said back. 'It's out of your hands. Now we do it my way.'

'Don't do anything stupid.'

'I did that over twelve years ago. It's payback time now. Your way was pointless. Maybe even lethal, as it's turned out. Now it's down to me again. This time I won't screw it up.'

Famous last words.

'What else could we have done?' he asked.

'Christ knows. But you couldn't have made a worse mess of this if you'd tried. There's only one way left now. Only one way to fight fire.'

'You'll have blood on your hands.'

'I already have enough of that, and it's hard to get it off,' I replied.

Slade was silent again for a moment, then he said, 'There's no way I can stop you, Sharman. But you'd better tell Toby that if he's not back in this office in an hour, he's finished with us.'

I looked over at Toby again, and told him what Slade had said. His only reply was to raise the middle finger of his left hand at the phone.

'I don't think he's too worried,' I said.

Slade changed tack. 'Where do *you* think she is?' he asked.

'With Collier of course. Where else?'

'Should we tell the police?'

'Please yourself.' I had toyed with the idea of telling Inspector Robber myself, and getting him in on the act, but I was past that by now. Like I'd said to Slade, there was only one way to fight fire. I was getting tired of trying to put it out by pissing on it.

'Listen, Slade,' I said. 'You do what you think is right, I'll do the same. If I've got anything interesting I'll be in touch, likewise if I need any information. Otherwise, forget you knew me.' And I put down the phone, and switched it off.

I filled Toby in on the rest of the news. I saw his knuckles gleam white through the skin on the back of his hands as he gripped the steering wheel hard.

'What do we do?' he asked.

'Fuck knows,' I said. 'But there must be something.'

43

We sat outside Collier's place for hours. Then I made Toby drive round the plot. I sensed that Collier wouldn't go far from his own ground. He was a desperate man by then. He had to be, to kidnap Jackie and try to blackmail a national newspaper.

The only problem was, how desperate?

He'd come close to killing before, and I wondered how long it would be before that particular course of action was the only option left open to him.

I told Toby to make a diversion to Croydon to give Millar's gaff a scan. It looked quiet enough, and there was no sign of his car. I toyed with the idea of sending Toby in for a recce, but nished it. He wasn't there. I could just tell.

We drove back towards Peckham as the boozers were letting out. Meat wagons full of Old Bill were screaming around the streets, with their sirens wailing. People were abusing each other outside the pubs and clubs, chip shops and mini-cab offices. They looked subhuman in the light from the street-lamps, and the puddles of vomit in the gutters took on the colour of blood. All in all, just another ordinary night in paradise.

We parked up again just down the street from Collier's house, and I took a swift look-see. It was as quiet as it had been earlier. I sat on the bonnet of the Merc and lit a cigarette. I caught sight of the image of myself in the mirror of a darkened shop window opposite, and I hardly recognised it as me. I looked like a casualty of war.

In the black glass of the shop front, behind me and the Mercedes, and the terrace of houses on the other side of the road where we were parked, lit up like an ocean-going liner, I saw the reflection of a tower block of flats, and I turned round and looked up at it, looming over me like some brightly lit leviathan, and suddenly something clicked.

I ran back round to the passenger side of the car and got in. 'Do you know a place called the Lion Estate?' I said to Toby.

'Never heard of it.'

'You're about to get an education. Take the first on the left.'

Going back on to the estate wasn't a pleasant experience for me. I remembered the last time I'd been there, and a cold sweat broke out under my arms, and trickled down my sides under my shirt. I licked my lips and touched the gun in my pocket for reassurance again.

Toby bounced the Merc over the sleeping policeman at the entrance to the Lion and drove slowly towards the block where Sailor Grant had died.

There were a few groups of people hanging out on street corners, and they clocked the Mercedes well as it drove by.

'They'll remember us,' commented Toby.

'Don't worry,' I said. 'They just think we're crack dealers doing our rounds.'

He steered the car around to the front of the block and, just as he was pulling up to the kerb, the front door was pushed open and a familiar figure appeared. It was my old mate Detective Sergeant Millar.

'Drive on,' I hissed. 'Don't make it obvious.'

Toby touched the accelerator with his toe, and the Merc slid round the corner into the darkness at the side of the building. I looked over my shoulder and watched as DS Millar made his way to a Ford Sierra parked in the shadows opposite.

'That's one of them,' I said.

'It's one of the two who took Jackie,' confirmed Toby, and he made to get out of the car.

I grabbed his arm and tugged him back. 'Not so bloody fast,' I said.

'Why not?'

'There's plenty of time for him later. Let him go.'

Reluctantly, Toby stayed where he was, as Millar crossed the road.

'Do you think Jackie's inside?' asked Toby.

'I'd put money on it.'

We waited until the Sierra pulled away, then got out of the Mercedes.

'Let's take a look,' I said. 'And stay cool. If she is there it means that Collier's upstairs. Maybe another copper – Grisham. He's with the Sweeney. So be careful. Don't forget we've got the element of surprise on our side.'

We took the stairs up to the sixth floor, just like I'd done the last time I went calling. The ambience hadn't improved any, since.

As we went, I described the inside of the flat as far as I could recall it, which wasn't a lot, but might be useful. When we got to the landing, all we could hear was someone's sound system on the floor above, playing techno-dub reggae at a volume that was almost shaking the building off its foundations.

I pulled Toby close and shouted in his ear. 'That door there –' indicating number 22 '– how we going to play this?'

He reached under his arm and pulled a Browning Hi-Power 9mm automatic from its holster, and chambered a shell. Then from the pocket of his jacket he extracted a silencer. A nine-inch length of silver pipe with a satin finish, and screwed it into the barrel of the pistol.

'Hardly need this,' he shouted back, jerking his thumb upwards towards the source of the music. 'But what the hell? I take out the door and go in first. You follow me and give me cover.' I hoped it was Collier inside and not Sailor's mate enjoying a late-night snack of beans on toast.

'Don't shoot anyone unless you have to,' I said, and drew the Commando and cocked it.

He gave me a circle with the thumb and forefinger of his left hand, and walked to number 22 and fired three times at the lock. The wood around it blew apart and the door sagged open. He glanced at me, gave me the same sign and went inside. I followed him into the stench I remembered so well.

Toby ran ahead of me, the automatic in a two-handed grip, fanning the corridor and the inside of the living room where I'd been given such a beating. I stayed by the front door in the wash of sound from above. Then simultaneously, the record ended, leaving an empty silence almost as loud as the music had been, the door to the bathroom opened, and Collier appeared, zipping up his flies.

I stuck the barrel of the Colt into his neck and said, 'Just keep your hands where they are, son, the party's over.'

He did as he was told, and his eyes darted from me to Toby and back.

'Where is she?' I demanded.

'Who?'

I hit him in the face then, right across the bridge of the nose with the gun. Like I said, I was getting fed up with pissing about. Blood leaked out of his nostrils and he went to put his hand up to them.

'Leave it,' I said. 'You can drown for all I care.'

He gave me such a look of pure hatred as I've never had before or since, but I managed to live with it.

'Jacqueline Harvey,' I said. 'Where is she?'

'Back bedroom,' he said. His voice was thick, and he leant his head back against the wall and sucked blood out of his sinuses.

'Anybody else here?'

Collier shook his head, and a snake of blood flew across his cheek.

'Toby, keep him covered,' I said, then to Collier, 'Got a handkerchief?'

'Side pocket,' he replied.

I reached in and fished out a neatly folded linen square and gave it to him. He gingerly put it against his nose.

'Put your other hand on the back of your neck,' I ordered.

He did so, and I frisked him thoroughly from head to toe. Toby kept the Browning cocked and pointed at Collier's head all the time. In a belt holster on Collier's left side I found a Smith & Wesson

Model 12 Police Airweight with a two-inch barrel that I stuffed into the pocket of my jacket.

'Armed and dangerous,' I said. 'I hope you've got a licence for this.'

He didn't reply.

'In there,' I said to him, pointing towards the living room. 'Toby, go and find Jackie. I'll keep this one company. Be careful, I don't trust the fucker. There might be someone with her.'

Toby walked down the hall, carefully opening doors as he went, and I followed Collier into the room where I'd nearly died.

Like the stairway, it hadn't changed much either in the interim. But I felt that I had. I told him to sit on the orange crate, and keep one hand on his nose, and put the other on his knee and keep it there.

He did as he was told, but his eyes were still full of hate, and I knew there was only one way this was going to finish.

'When's Millar coming back?' I asked.

'Tomorrow morning.'

I didn't know if he was lying or not.

'You'd better be telling me the truth,' I warned him.

He made some sort of noise into the handkerchief that could have meant anything.

A minute later Toby and Jackie came into the room. She looked pale and dishevelled, but nothing worse.

'Are you all right?' I said.

She nodded, then walked over to Collier and kicked him hard on one shin. He winced at the pain. It wasn't his night.

Right then, the music from above started up again.

Shit, I thought.

Jackie came close, and shouted in my ear. 'It's quieter at the back.'

I nodded, gestured for Collier to stand up, and pushed him through the door and along the hall. The flat was a lot bigger than I thought. It went right round the side of the building, and by the time we got to the kitchen it was possible to talk above the sound of the music without bawling at one another. Not that the kitchen was somewhere you'd want to spend a lot of time. The sink had leaked all over the floor, and the stove looked like it hadn't been cleaned since the Lion had been built. But at least there were a couple of chairs to sit on. I put Collier in one, and Jackie sat on the other.

'Did they hurt you?' I asked her.

'What them? No. Not so's you'd notice. Don't forget I've been hurt by experts.'

'I know the feeling,' I said.

'So what do we do now?' asked Toby.

'We get Jackie as far away from here as possible. Out of the country. There's a lot more shit due to hit the fan before this lot's all over.'

They didn't know the half of it.

'Is that all right with you, Jackie?' I asked. 'A holiday in the sun. With Toby.'

She looked shyly at him. 'It sounds good,' she said.

'Good,' I said. Then to Toby, 'Have you got any money?'

He frowned. 'Just a little.' Then his face brightened. 'But I've got the company's plastic.' He hesitated. 'But I don't think I work for them any more, do I?'

'I shouldn't worry about that,' I said. 'I'll straighten it out. Have you got your passport?'

Toby tapped his jacket. 'Always,' he said.

'Good. Jackie?'

'It's at my flat.'

'Right. Toby, you take Jackie to her place. Grab her passport and get to Heathrow. Get on to the first plane to somewhere warm. Preferably somewhere they don't get English papers for a week or so. Don't go near Fortescue's. Use your card to buy what you need when you get wherever you're going. Tell no one, and I mean no one, where you are. Just go. In a couple of weeks phone Slade. I think everything will be cool by then. All sorted. One way or another.'

'What about you?' said Jackie.

'I'll be OK.' I looked at my watch. It was almost one a.m. 'I'll stay here with Collier till morning. Give you plenty of time to get the first flight out. Then I'll let Slade know he can print, and no one will be damned.'

Just me probably, I thought.

'Now go,' I said. 'Get lost. And have a good time.'

Jackie came over and kissed me on the cheek, and there were tears in her eyes. 'Thank you,' she said. 'For everything.'

'No worries,' I replied. 'Take care of yourself, you hear?'

'Thank you,' she said again. 'I'll never forget you. I'll pray for you each night.'

It was nice to know that someone would.

'Go,' I said. 'And good luck.'

Toby shook my hand. 'Are you sure you'll be OK?' he asked.

'Course I will.'

'But you've got no car.'

'I'll be fine,' I said. 'I'm a big boy now.'

He slapped me on the back, and took Jackie's arm and led her out of the kitchen. She looked back once, and smiled, but I saw the same look in her eyes that I'd seen all those years before at Brixton nick.

Then it was just me and Collier. And the DJ upstairs.

44

I sat in the rickety chair that Jackie had vacated opposite Collier, and looked at him. He wasn't so much, bleeding nose and all, with his handkerchief, all black with blood, stuck up against it.

'So, Terry,' I said. 'Just you and me.'

He took his hankie off his face and said through swollen lips, 'I'm going to get you for this.'

The melodrama of the remark should have been funny, but it wasn't. 'Don't you ever give up?' I asked. 'It's over, son. *Finito*. The end of an era. You've had a good run for your money. Why don't you just give in gracefully?'

He sneered, and spat out a gob of blood which landed between my feet.

'There's no getting through to you, is there?' I asked. 'No getting through to you at all.'

'I'm going to kill you, Sharman,' Collier said. And I believed he would if I gave him half a chance. 'I should've finished the job the last time.'

'You stupid shit,' I said. 'You shouldn't even have told me that Sailor was dead. I would never have known and, even if I did, so what? I didn't care one way or another who murdered Carol Harvey after all this time, God help me. It was history. But you had to stir it all up again.'

'Grant told me you were going to help him.'

'Do what?'

'I looked him up at the address he gave after he got out. It was his uncle's. He told me you were going to help him. Then he went on the run.'

'Who could blame him?' I said. 'With you on his tail again. And he ended up here, poor fucker. So that's why he killed himself. Because he was scared of you.'

And I never gave him a chance to tell me.

'But you were going to have a meeting with Grant,' he said. 'He told me.'

'Then he was lying. Maybe he thought you'd leave him alone if he said that.' Fat chance, I thought. 'I only agreed to meet him after he'd left his uncle's. And that was just to get him off my back. He kept phoning me up, whingeing and whining about how hard done by he'd been. I told him to fuck off when I did see him. I told you that the last time we were here. But you wouldn't have it, would you? And now look where you are. You're finished, son. You and Millar and Grisham and Byrne. When that paper comes out on Sunday, you are fucked.'

'Not so fucked that I can't get someone to deal with you.'

'Like you were going to deal with Jackie?'

'Another few minutes and I would've.'

'How did you find her at the hotel, by the way? She wasn't supposed to tell anyone.'

'I went knocking on doors around where she lived. Showing my warrant. She'd left the keys of her flat with some bird a couple of doors down. She's got goldfish, see. Jackie. Can you believe this? She left her address with the bird in case something happened to the fish.'

Fucking fish, I thought. I don't believe I'm hearing this.

'Oh well,' I said. 'It's all over now.'

'Don't you believe it. It won't be over till I see you dead.'

'There's only one thing to do then.'

'What?'

'I'll have to kill *you*, son. That's all there is to it. It won't be over till one of us *is* dead. That's for sure.'

This town isn't big enough for the two of us, I thought. Just like the old westerns I used to watch at Saturday morning pictures.

'You haven't got the bottle,' said Collier.

'We'll see about that,' I replied. But I wasn't sure that he was far wrong. 'Come on, let's go into the other room. It's noisier in there, and no one'll hear the shots.'

He went a bit cross-eyed at that, and didn't move. So I got up and went over and grabbed his lapel, hauled him to his feet and pushed him out into the hall. I shoved him along, and reluctantly he went.

We were about halfway down the length of it when I felt a presence behind me, and something hard was pushed into my back. A voice I recognised said, 'Drop it.'

It was Millar. He'd stepped out of one of the rooms off the corridor, and if it wasn't a gun barrel poking into my back, it was a pretty fair approximation.

I stood still with the Colt pointing at Collier. Then I heard the unmistakable click of a firearm's hammer being cocked behind me. 'Don't fuck about, Sharman,' said Millar. 'Or I'll blow your kidneys away.'

Shit, I thought, as Collier turned and grabbed the Colt out of my hand, and poked it into my face. 'Cunt,' he said and punched me left-handed in the side of my jaw.

I felt blood of my own in my mouth, and he reached into my jacket pocket and retrieved the Smith & Wesson I'd taken off him earlier.

'Your turn,' he said. 'In the big room. You're dead, you slag.'

So that was that. The tables were well and truly turned, and I knew that this time the only way I'd leave the flat was in a body bag.

I felt my bowels go liquid, and I cursed my own stupidity. Still, it was too late for that. Far too late.

Slowly I walked in front of the pair of them towards the living room of the flat.

'What happened, guv'nor?' asked Millar, as we went. 'Where did he spring from?'

'Fuck knows,' replied Collier. 'He turned up with the bird's boyfriend. Fuckers caught me in the kazi.'

'Where is she now?'

'Gone to the airport with the bloke. Don't worry. There's no planes till morning. We'll catch up with them.'

Bastard, I thought, and my head spun with ways to get out of my predicament, but I couldn't come up with one that had a ghost of a chance of working.

Millar pushed me into the middle of the room, and stood on my left, holding a small, but lethal, Colt revolver of his own.

Collier walked round to face me. He stuck my Colt in his jacket pocket, and bellowed, 'How did you find out about Byrne's confession?'

'You told me.'

He looked at me in disbelief. 'When?'

'In the car, after you beat me up in here. When you were taking me up the marshes to kill me. You must've thought I was out of it.'

'We did, otherwise you would never've got out of the motor. So you never saw it. It was all a bluff what they were going to write in the paper.'

'Papers like that don't bluff,' I said. 'There's too much at stake. They saw it all right. Or at least a copy.'

'How did you get it?'

I had to smile – even under the circumstances. 'How's the alarm system at your place? Had it fixed yet?'

He looked puzzled.

'A bit of damp in the junction box, wasn't it?' I said.

I saw realisation dawn on him. 'That was you?'

'Me and someone else. We got in, found your safe and I made a couple of copies.'

'You scumbag.'

'You can talk,' I said. 'When it comes to being scum, you've got anyone else I know beat by a mile.'

I thought he was going to hit me again, but he just smiled in triumph. 'Keep talking, Sharman,' he said. 'Keep flapping your gums. You've had it, my son. Had it good and proper.'

That was fair enough. As long as we were talking, I was still alive. And like they always say, where there's life there's hope – not much, but a bit.

'Tell me something,' I said. 'Just one last thing.'

'What?'

'How come you believed Jacqueline Harvey that day in Brixton, and not Byrne? How come you sussed out that he'd raped Carol?'

'What, old Alan Byrne? Good old Al. Simple. I'd known him a long time. A lot of years. And I knew what he liked.'

'What?'

'Young girls, mate. They were his weakness. Not as young as Carol and Jacqueline, I'll grant you. But young enough. I'd seen him at our do's. Always with a stripper on his knee. The younger the better. And magazines. He had quite a collection. Used to get them from the porn squad. I wasn't surprised. I knew his missus too. She was like a prune left out in the sun. If I'd been him, I'd've gone for some sweet young meat as well. When I went back and saw him after young Jacqueline had gone, he was all over the place. Shaking and sweating and all sorts. I put it to him that he'd done the deed. He folded like a wet rag. Pathetic. He was more worried about his promotion prospects than his nieces. I nearly done for him, I swear. But he begged me. Told me he'd help me and Millar and Grisham in the future, if we'd put someone in the frame for the rape. He'd do anything he said. I knew he was going to do well, and I agreed. What did I care about Carol Harvey? His only worry was that she'd wake up and shop him. I think he'd meant to kill her all along. But even if she did he thought that he'd be all right. That he'd got her so scared she wouldn't talk. When she died it was even easier. No witnesses, see. Byrne fell over himself to sign that confession. He'd've sucked my cock if I'd told him to. And we had Grant banged up ready to be charged, thanks to you and Lenny. Who was going to believe a nonce like that against all of us?'

'Me maybe,' I said.

'Which was why we never webbed you in. I never trusted you from the first minute I saw you.'

'Thank Christ for that,' I said. 'Being trusted by you isn't exactly a compliment to anyone's integrity.'

He raised his arm to hit me again, and Millar interjected, 'Come on, guv. Let's get it over with and out of here. We've got things to do.'

Collier looked at him and nodded. 'Right, Lenny,' he said. Then to me, 'Kneel down.'

'Do what?'

'You heard. Kneel down.'

'Fuck you,' I said defiantly, and Millar crashed his gun down on to my shoulder so hard that I thought my collar-bone had fractured.

'Down,' said Collier again.

I knew that if I didn't obey, they'd just beat me down, so I did as Collier ordered. I knelt on the dirty plastic-covered floor and looked up at him.

He cocked the S&W he was holding, and stuck it into my face. From my viewpoint, it looked as big and deadly as a cannon.

'Open your mouth,' he said.

I shook my head, and he slapped my face hard with his empty hand. 'Open it.'

I parted my lips, and he pushed the barrel of his gun hard against my teeth and smiled. 'Goodbye, Sharman,' he said, and I saw the knuckle of his trigger finger whiten.

So that's it, I thought. The sum total. My whole life lived for this. Kneeling on the floor of a stinking room, in a stinking flat, on a stinking estate, in a stinking town, having my head blown off my shoulders by a psychopathic copper. Jesus. What a way for it all to end. I'd thought about dying so often in the past, and begged for it to happen enough times, God knows, that maybe Collier was doing me a favour.

Perhaps now I'd get a bit of peace at last.

I looked past the gun in his hand, up into his face. My killer's face. The last face I'd ever see. And as the music from upstairs thumped on, I saw his head implode as a bullet entered just beneath his right eye, and blew out the back of his skull in a spray of blood, bone and brains. I felt something hot splash across my face, as his left eye popped out from the concussion of the entry, and more blood flew out of the empty socket. He stepped back, taking the gun away from my mouth, and fell to the floor. I looked at Millar, whose eyes widened, and whose head turned towards the door, before a second bullet slammed into his torso, then another, and another, raising dust from the material of his coat. He stumbled sideways, then he too fell to the floor and lay still, leaking blood from the entry holes.

I stayed where I was, then turned and looked round. Toby was standing in the doorway, holding his silenced Browning. He was wreathed in smoke, and a wisp escaped from the barrel of the silencer. The room stank of used gunpowder and blood and fear.

I put my hands on the floor in front of me, lowered my head, and breathed deeply, trying hard not to throw up.

'Are you OK?' he shouted above the sound of the reggae.

I've been better, I thought, but managed a swift nod.

He came over and dragged me to my feet. 'I saw the other one coming back as we were leaving. I had to make sure you were all right.'

I held on to Toby's shoulder for support. 'I'm glad you did,' I screamed above the constant noise. 'Where's Jackie?'

'In the car downstairs.'

Thank God, I thought. All she needed was to see this. 'Good,' I said.

Toby looked round the room and put his mouth close to my ear. 'We'd better get this mess cleared up,' he said.

'No,' I replied. 'You get out of here. Carry on as planned. Don't tell Jackie what happened. Just go.'

'But –'

'No buts. I owe you a biggie, Toby. I'll get this sorted. Now hop it. And give me your gun. I'll get rid of it.'

He handed me the still-hot pistol, and I put it on top of the orange crate.

'Go,' I shouted.

He nodded, then came over and took my hand again. 'Clean up your face,' he said, then shook my mitten, and left without looking back.

Maybe there was something to be said for SAS training, I thought as he went.

I walked into the bathroom and looked at my face in the sliver of filthy mirror above the hand basin. If I'd thought I looked like a casualty of war earlier, now I looked like a corpse. The skin of my face was white and grainy with black shadows under my eyes, and a streak of dark blood across my cheek. I ran some rusty water into my cupped hands and splashed the blood off, then dried myself with my fingers. The blood had hit the shoulder of my jacket and I rubbed it into the leather, which was already scuffed and stained enough so that one more dirty mark wouldn't matter. I looked into my eyes again before I left. I knew that my soul was already scuffed and stained too, and I wondered how many more dirty marks it could take before it wouldn't matter either.

I shrugged at my reflection, and went and cleaned up as best I could the room where Collier and Millar's bodies lay.

I found the four cartridge cases that Toby's Browning had ejected and stuck them into the pocket of my jeans. Then I recovered my Colt Commando from Collier's pocket and stuck it into my belt in the small of my back. I put Collier's S&W in one pocket of my jacket and Millar's Colt in the other. Then I unscrewed the silencer from Toby's automatic, and put it in one pocket and the Browning in the other.

I had so many guns on me that I felt like a walking ordnance depot.

In the corridor outside the flat I found the three cartridge cases that had been used to blow away the lock, and I put them in my pocket with the rest.

Then I left.

45

I went downstairs, and ducked through the shadows to the edge of the estate. I hardly saw a soul as I went. The night air was cool and soothing on the skin of my face, and once I was on the main road I just kept walking. I'd considered taking Millar's Sierra, but I left it. The thought of driving a dead man's wheels wasn't very appealing. And besides, I'd have to lose it somewhere, and I didn't want it on my local ground.

As I walked, I wondered what I'd do if I got a pull from Old Bill. Run? Surrender? Shoot it out? But as it happened, I didn't see any trace of law at all.

I walked from New Cross, through Nunhead, taking a cut across the cemetery, then over Peckham Rye to Dulwich, and down to Herne Hill. The streets were practically empty, and the traffic lights reflected red and amber and green on to the hard, bare tarmac that was rainbowed blue and pink with petrol as I went. By that time it was almost four a.m., and my bad foot was killing me, so I caught a cruising cab to my place.

I knew I'd never be able to sleep, so I unplugged the phone and sat in the chair by the window, smoking cigarettes, drinking beer and waiting for it to get light. I wanted to give Toby and Jackie plenty of time to get out of the country. Around seven I went to my local greasy for breakfast.

I phoned Slade from the café.

'Where the hell have you been?' he demanded.

'Around and about,' I replied.

'What's happening?'

'We found Jacqueline Harvey. She's safe. You can print the story now.'

Not that it made all that much difference any more. Fate had intervened and taken two of the leading characters out of the game. But at least it would nail Byrne's stinking hide out to dry, and let the world know exactly what kind of man he really was. And, of course, there was Grisham. Another dirty copper. And it would clear Sailor Grant's name. Not that I thought there was anyone in the world who would care too much about that. But maybe, somewhere, Sailor's spirit could finally get some sort of rest.

'What happened? Who took her, and where?' demanded Slade.

'It doesn't matter.'

'Yes it does.'

'Not to me. It'll all come out sooner or later. I'm getting tired of the whole thing.' *And* I knew it wasn't finished yet.

'I'm not.'

'Mr Slade, I really couldn't care less.'

'I want to know,' he insisted. 'You owe me that.'

I knew he could smell more of a story, but I'd given him all I was going to. 'Too bad. And I don't think I owe you anything.'

I couldn't believe I was having this conversation. Not so soon after nearly being killed, then seeing two men gunned down in front of my eyes. So close that I was spattered with blood still warm from Collier's body.

I started to get a late reaction then, and my body trembled from head to toe and I had to push the telephone receiver hard against my ear to keep it still.

'You'll find out in time,' I said. 'It'll make an interesting sidebar. Really interesting, believe me.'

He changed the subject suddenly. Maybe he realised that I wasn't going to cough any more right then. 'Where is Jacqueline Harvey now?' he asked.

'A long way from here, I hope,' I replied.

'But where?'

'I don't know.'

'What do you mean, you don't know?'

'Exactly what I say, for Chrissake. Do I have to spell everything out? I sent her away. She was on the first flight out of Heathrow this morning to anywhere but here.'

'She's out of the country? What the hell did you tell her to leave the country for?'

'You'll find out,' I said.

'And where's Toby Gillis?'

'He's with her.'

'*What*?'

'I told him to take care of her. He's using the paper's plastic. No one ever asked for money for this story, although I know there was cash available. Things have changed in a big way.' I didn't elaborate. All that would come out later, and I'd worry about it when it did. 'And I told Toby to get her as far away as possible. You can find out easily where they've gone, but don't. Not for a few days. She's done her bit, and she deserves some peace.'

'Gillis is no longer employed by this company,' Slade said stiffly. 'He knew the consequences of not reporting to the office last night.'

'Don't be such a prat, Slade,' I said. 'Rehire him. Forget you fired him. Take my word that he earned his money last night. Do what has to be done, but keep Toby on.'

Slade didn't say anything.

'Well?' I said into the silence at the other end of the line.

'All right. But I'll need to talk to him.'

'Check his credit card bills. You'll find him. But I told him to get as far away from civilisation as possible, so it might take a few days.'

'I should cancel the bloody card.'

'Then you won't find him at all. Use your loaf.'

'I suppose,' said Slade. 'But I wish you'd tell me exactly what's going on.'

'All in good time.'

'You should have been a journalist,' said Slade. 'You're close-mouthed enough. And persuasive enough.'

'So, you'll go with the story?'

'Of course – if what you're telling me, or rather what you're *not* telling me, is as hot as you say.'

'It is.'

'So I go with the story. But if you're lying...'

'As if,' I said. As if I cared, I thought. There was nothing that he could do to me that was worse than had already been done.

'Tell me something,' I said.

'What?'

'What time does the first edition of the paper hit the streets tonight?'

'The first run comes off the presses at about nine.'

'Fine.'

'Why?'

'Just interested.'

'Read it in good health,' said Slade.

That was a joke. 'I will,' I said. 'And I'll be in touch.' I hung up.

All I could manage at the café was a cup of tea. Then I went home. On the way I dropped the seven cartridge cases and the silencer from Toby Gillis's Browning down the first drain I passed. When I got back, I stashed Collier and Millar's guns in my hiding place under the roof of the house, and sat at the table in my flat, where, after pulling on a pair of cotton gloves, I broke Toby's gun into its component parts and carefully cleaned each one. I reassembled it, and put it into a plastic bag which I hid under the mattress on my bed.

For the rest of the day I sat indoors listening to the news every hour on the radio to hear if Collier and Millar's bodies had been discovered.

They hadn't.

46

At seven-thirty that evening I phoned Doug Harvey, Jackie and Carol's father. I hadn't been looking forward to the call, but I'd promised Jackie. I left it as late as possible. He answered on the third ring. 'Mr Harvey,' I said.

'Who wants to know?'

'My name is Nick Sharman. I don't know if you remember me. I was a DC at Brixton nick when your daughter Carol was murdered twelve years ago.'

There was nothing but silence at the end of the line. Then I heard him catch his breath. 'So?'

'We spoke a couple of times then. I was in on the arrest of the man Grant who went to prison for the murder. And I met you again at the trial.'

'I remember.'

'This is difficult,' I said. 'But Grant came out of prison this summer and got in touch with me. Until he signed the confession that got him put away, he always protested his innocence. And I believed him. Well, I don't know, I wasn't sure... whatever. He *thought* I believed him.'

'So?' said Harvey again.

'Grant wanted me to help him prove he was innocent after all this time. I'm a private detective now. I refused. I didn't want to get involved. But two policemen, Collier and Millar – you must remember them; they were on the original case too – heard that Grant had got in touch with me when he got out, and they thought I was sticking my nose into their business, and they tried to dissuade me.'

'How?'

'They put me into hospital. It's a long story. It doesn't matter now. When I came out of hospital, I dug around a bit. I met your daughter Jackie. Jacqueline.'

He didn't say a word.

'She told me certain things. Things about your brother-in-law, Alan Byrne.'

'What kind of things?'

I didn't answer right away. It was almost too painful.

'This is very hard for me to tell you, Mr Harvey. But she told me that, ever since your wife died, up until the time of the murder, Alan Byrne had been sexually assaulting Jacqueline and her sister.'

I heard him sob.

'Do you want to meet me, Mr Harvey? We shouldn't discuss this on the phone.'

I heard him take in breath again. 'Tell me,' he said.

'Jacqueline also told me that Carol was going to tell you what had been happening. Alan Byrne got her to go to Brixton that afternoon and raped her for the last time. And killed her to keep her quiet.'

'Oh Christ… No,' said Harvey.

'Jacqueline told Detective Sergeant Collier what had really happened. Byrne denied it of course, and scared Jacqueline into changing her story. Collier didn't believe him, or her, when she *did* change her story. But instead of taking criminal proceedings against Byrne, he beat a confession out of Grant, who we had in for questioning. It was the day we talked at Brixton. Do you remember?'

If I'd expected a reaction, I was disappointed.

'It was a beating that I witnessed,' I went on. 'Or at least most of it. That night Grant signed his confession. Then, after Carol died and the charge became murder, Collier got your brother-in-law to sign a confession of his own. A confession that Collier kept ever since. And as far as I can make out, when Grant was safely away inside,

Collier used that confession to blackmail Alan Byrne. A little bit of promotion for him, Millar and a DI named Grisham – you probably remember him too; he was on the case with the rest of us – and *carte blanche* for the three of them to do virtually as they pleased. It hasn't all come out yet. Byrne was a high flyer. With him in their pocket…' I didn't bother to finish. Doug Harvey knew what his brother-in-law was.

'What about you?' asked Harvey. His voice was hoarse and guttural.

'I wasn't included. I'd already rocked the boat too much, telling people I thought Grant was innocent. In *that* case at least. Collier and Millar and Grisham didn't want to know about me after that. Eventually I transferred away, then came back to Brixton, and got involved in some dodgy business of my own. I took early retirement on medical grounds.'

'So why are you telling me all this now? And where's Jacqueline?'

'I'm telling you now, because Grant killed himself a while back. The same day Collier and Millar gave me the beating that put me into hospital. They nearly killed me. And to be frank, I could never consider myself safe from them until the truth was known. I introduced Jacqueline to a journalist who freelances for a Sunday paper.' I told him which one. 'Tomorrow, the story comes out. They're not naming names. Not at first. There's already been an injunction threatened by your brother-in-law's lawyers. The paper's ignoring the threat. And later tonight, the news editor of the paper is passing the file of evidence that's been gathered to the police for them to take further action. There's a straight copper's been interested in the case since I was beaten. A bloke called Robber, an inspector at Gipsy Hill. I told Slade, that's the news editor, to give the stuff straight to him.'

'*What?*' said Harvey in amazement.

'It's true I'm afraid.'

'And where's Jacqueline now? Why isn't she telling me all this?'

'There was some trouble. What isn't important. It's over now. I sent Jacqueline away with a friend of hers. I don't know where they've gone. Somewhere far away. Somewhere she can get some peace. She couldn't find it in herself to tell you.'

'And the paper's coming out tomorrow?' was all he said.

'That's right.'

'Jesus. And you say that this Inspector Robber gets the information later tonight.'

'Correct. After the first edition's out on the street.'

The line was silent for a moment.

'Are you still there?' I asked.

'I'm here.'

'Do you want me to come over, Mr Harvey? We could talk.'

'*You?* No, you stay away. You started all this. I need time to think.' And he put the phone down.

I started all this. Well isn't that always the way?

The receiver I was holding was slick with sweat, and I could feel rivers of it running down my side. I didn't ever want to make another call like that in my life.

I drank some water and lit a cigarette, then drove up to the print works in Wapping. I took the Colt Commando and Toby's Browning for company.

I arrived about half past eight, and got stopped by two heavy-duty security goons at the barbed-wire-covered front gate.

They both came out of their hut and walked over to the driver's side of my car. I could tell they didn't like me from the off.

'Is Tom Slade about?' I asked.

One of the goons looked at the other, then back at me, and said, 'Do what?'

Typical.

'Tom Slade,' I said. 'News editor.'

'Who are you?'

'Nick Sharman.'

'Got an appointment?'

I shook my head. 'But I think he'll want to see me, so why don't you run along and find out,' I said.

I suppose I could have pulled out my gun and shot my way in, but I thought that a more low-key approach might be better.

'Wait here,' said one of the goons and went back into his box and made a call.

When he came out he didn't look too happy, but swallowed it, and said, 'Drive on through. There's a car park about five hundred yards on your left. Park in one of the spaces marked "Visitor". You'll be met.'

'I know where the car park is,' I said. 'I've been here before.' If I thought that would give me some cachet, I was wrong. They didn't seem very impressed at the information, and both went back into the hut; the gate opened slowly in front of me, and I did as I was told.

I found the car park and made for the door I'd entered the last time. Just as I reached it, the same young woman I'd met before opened it and said, 'Hello. Tom's with the rest of the editorial team.' She led me through a maze of corridors and left me in an empty office with only a coffee machine for company. 'He won't be a minute,' she said.

And he wasn't. He appeared about thirty seconds later carrying a pile of newspapers.

'This is why you're here, I suppose?' he said, holding up the papers.

I took one of them from him, and said, 'That's right.'

I scoped the front page. It held a massive banner headline: 'EX-TOP COP IN MURDER SCANDAL'. Beneath it, in slightly smaller type, was printed: 'Metropolitan Police officers covered up his guilt. Innocent man jailed for twelve years.' I read the story quickly. It was continued on pages two and three. Like Slade had said, no names were mentioned. But the places and dates were correct. Nice touch that. Anyone who wanted to check old newspaper files could come up with the facts in a minute. There was one photo of Jacqueline Harvey, taken at the Fortescue, with her eyes blocked out in black.

'Did you get in touch with Jack Robber?' I asked.

Slade nodded. 'He's meeting with our legal people in an hour or so. They have all the information that we do, and will give it to him then.'

'Good,' I said. 'Old Jack will have a field day.'

He nodded.

'Can I have those?' I said, indicating the rest of the papers he was holding.

Slade shrugged and handed them over. 'Are you happy with it?' he asked.

I shook my head. 'What's there to be happy about?' I didn't know if I meant the story, or something bigger. Life maybe. But that was too big a ball of wax to think about right then.

'Do you want to tell me the rest now?'

I shook my head. The bastard never gave up.

'We've located Jacqueline Harvey and Toby Gillis,' said Slade, after a moment when I didn't answer. 'They flew to Nassau, then rented a car and booked into a hotel.'

'And?' I asked.

'I'm sending someone over to talk to them tomorrow. I thought I'd give them some time alone.'

'How magnanimous of you.'

'I don't think I like your tone.'

'Jesus,' I said. 'I'm crushed.' And without another word, I left.

I drove across to Dulwich. It didn't take long. The lights were on in Detective Inspector Paul Grisham's house, and I saw him behind undrawn curtains in the living room. I took one of the papers off the seat beside me and walked up the drive, where a new Saab was parked facing the garage doors. I rang the bell at the front door and he answered. He looked at me standing there, and he didn't know who the hell I was. It had been a long time – a long time for both of us.

'Hello, Paul,' I said. 'Remember me?'

He sort of shook his head like people do, then I saw recognition behind his eyes. 'Sharman?' he said.

'Right first time.'

'What do you want?'

'I wanted to show you this,' I said, and handed him the paper I was holding. He squinted at the front page in the hall light. 'Christ,' he said, then turned to pages two and three and said 'Christ' again, then looked up at me.

'What the fuck is all this about?'

'Isn't it obvious?' I asked. 'The skeletons have started rattling in the cupboard.'

'Someone said a reporter tried to get me on the phone...'

'You should have called back,' I said.

He held the paper in one hand and said, 'But what does it all mean?' He looked as if he'd aged ten years since answering the door.

'It means it's all up, Paul,' I said. 'They know everything.'

'No one knows *everything*,' he replied.

Pretty profound for someone looking ruin in the face, I thought.

'Aren't you going to invite me in?' I asked.

After a heartbeat or two, he stepped back to allow me entry.

I followed him into the living room. He walked over to the windows, and drew the curtains tightly.

There was a quarter-empty bottle of Scotch on the table, and a single glass next to it, half full.

'Want a drink?' he asked.

'I'm choosy who I drink with,' I said.

'You never used to be.' He picked up the glass and took a sip.

'I never used to be lots of things.'

'Collier should have killed you when he had a chance,' he said.

'You know about that?'

He nodded. 'I know. Collier always kept me informed about what was going on.'

'That was good of him.'

'He liked to keep in touch. Liked to make sure that I never forgot what we did together. As if I would.'

'Did you ever have a reunion? I believe there's a nice little boozer next to the cemetery where Carol Harvey is buried.'

'You bastard.' He took another swallow from his glass. 'Yes. He should have killed you when he had a chance.'

'We all make mistakes,' I said.

He nodded. I think he knew that very well.

'So why don't you tell me about everything, Paul?' I asked. 'Before we decide what to do with you.'

'What do you mean?'

'You said just now that no one knows everything. Cast your mind back twelve years or so and tell me your version. Why you let the bastard that raped and murdered that girl go free, and helped bang up the poor pathetic sod who didn't.'

He licked his lips. 'It all happened so quickly. Collier made it sound easy.'

'You were his superior officer,' I said. 'You could have stopped him in a second. I always wondered why you let him take over that night.'

'It was Byrne. He made me. He knew some things about me.'

'Jesus Christ!' I exploded. 'Was everyone in that nick bent in those days?'

Grisham took another mouthful of Scotch. 'It was something and nothing. A misunderstanding. I thought it had all been forgotten. But Byrne kept the paperwork. I doubt if I would even have been reprimanded if it had come out. But it could have held up my promotion.'

'A backhander?'

'No. Nothing like that.' He sounded offended at the suggestion. 'I altered a statement. I knew the bloke was guilty –'

'A touch of the old verbals,' I interrupted.

'Something like that. He deserved to be put away. He would have been next time.'

'You just altered the timescale?'

He didn't know if I was being sarky or not.

'That's right.'

'So you'd had plenty of practice when it came to getting a bent confession out of Sailor Grant.'

He didn't reply.

'And because you were worried that you might have to wait another year or so for your promotion, you let that murderer stay out.'

'Do you think I haven't lived with that knowledge all this time? What it's done to me?'

'Spare me that. I'll be in bleedin' tears in a minute, and I haven't got any Kleenex with me.'

Now he *knew* I was being sarky.

He went on the attack then. 'And what about you?' he said. 'You're no better. You were there. You could have done something.'

'Sure. Just me against the four of you.' But of course he was right. And that was something *I* had to live with.

'And look at what you did in the end. That drugs thing. How can you judge me?' So he knew about that too. My fame had spread far and wide.

'Because no damned rapist and murderer went free because of what I did. And when I got collared, I took my medicine,' I said.

'You should have got five years.'

He was right again, of course. There was no arguing with that either. So I didn't. But I knew there was all the difference in the world between us.

'You're a prick, Paul. And you're finished,' I said, instead.

He didn't bother to argue any more. He must have seen the look in my eyes. 'What shall I do?' he asked.

'Get in your car and drive to the local nick. Tell them the lot. I'll come with you.'

'I'll phone Collier,' he said.

'It'll be a waste of a call.'

'Why?'

'Collier's dead. So's Millar.'

'Fuck. No.'

'Fuck. Yes.'

'You killed them?'

I shook my head. 'Not me. Someone else. Collier was trying to kill me.'

'Again? Christ, I didn't know.'

'No one does. Except us and the bloke who killed them. And he's long gone.'

'What about Byrne?'

'He's next on my list for a visit.'

'I'll call him.'

'No you won't, Paul. You won't call anyone. Like I said, you're finished. Do as I say. Go in and cough the lot. It'll make you feel better.'

He looked at me through red-rimmed eyes. 'I had to do it. You know that, don't you?'

'Bollocks,' I said. 'You were going for the main chance. You and

Collier and Millar – all of you. You all had a result out of it.'

God, when I thought of all the laws that had been broken by those four bastards: perverting the course of justice; perjury; kidnapping; false imprisonment; attempted murder; rape; underage sex; ABH; GBH. And how many more that I couldn't even think of? And then there was poor fucking Sailor. They stole his life in more ways than one. And all the people apart from him that had been screwed up to satisfy Byrne's lust for young girls, and the other three's lust for power: Carol Harvey; her sister Jacqueline; their father; Toby Gillis. And me.

'Just go, Paul,' I said tiredly. 'The first editions of the paper hit the street in a few hours. If you don't go to them, they'll be coming to you before morning.'

He picked up the glass of whisky and drained it.

'All right,' he said. 'I'm going.'

'I'll follow you in my car,' I said.

He nodded. It was all too easy; I should have known that something was up.

He collected his keys and left the house without turning off the lights. He got into the car parked in the driveway, and headed south. I followed.

Grisham didn't drive fast, and I kept up easily. Too easily. Coming up to Crystal Palace, he faked me out at a set of red lights, did a screaming, and highly illegal, turn over the central reservation, into the stream of traffic crossing in front of us, and left me blocked in by a BT van with my thumb firmly up my arse, listening to the sound of angry horns from the cars he'd cut up.

It was sheer luck I found him again. I was just cruising the streets. I decided that I'd waste another ten minutes looking, then head for Byrne's. I turned down a long, straight road that ran alongside a railway line, when I saw the Saab, parked neatly up beside the bottom of a pedestrian bridge over the tracks, with all the lights off.

I stopped behind it, turned off the engine of my car, opened the door and got out. I walked over to Grisham's motor and looked round for some sign of him. There was none.

I kicked at the ground, and decided to go up on the bridge to see if

I could spot him. As I climbed the steps, I saw him and stopped. He was leaning on the wall of the bridge looking down the line in the direction of central London. There was a lit lamp just above where he was standing, and I could see that he looked like warmed-over shit.

Then I heard it, far off in the distance, the two-tone klaxon of an inter-city express. He heard it too, and his expression changed, and I knew what he was going to do.

I remained where I was until I heard the sound of the train itself. I suppose I could have walked up the last few steps and said something to him. Tried to talk him out of what I knew he was going to do.

But I stayed where I was, as the train rounded a bend half a mile or so away from the bridge, and Grisham heaved himself up on to the edge of the parapet.

I think I could still have saved him. A shout might have done it or, on the other hand, made him do it earlier. I'll never know. As the train swept along towards us, he jumped, with a wild whoop. Of what? Triumph? Fear? Relief? Joy? Don't ask me. I didn't hear him hit the ground, or the train hit him, for the noise of the engine. All I heard was the scream from the wheels on the lines as the driver slammed on the brakes. I didn't look either. By then I didn't care.

I just went back down to my car and got behind the wheel.

47

I drove straight to Redhill. Every light in Byrne's huge house was on as the Jaguar crunched up the long gravel drive towards it. There were two cars parked on the turnaround in front of the building, and two men stood in the porch, their shadows long and black across the crushed white stone that sparkled in the spill from the house lights.

I stopped the E-Type, picked up a copy of the paper, got out and walked towards them.

Even with the light behind him, I recognised the bulk of Byrne standing in the doorway, and then with a start I realised that the man on the step below him was Doug Harvey. He half turned at my approach, and I saw a gun in his hand.

'Stop right there,' he ordered. 'Who are you?'

'It's me,' I said. 'Nick Sharman. We just spoke on the phone,' I added. As if he needed reminding.

'*You*,' he spat. 'I should have known you'd turn up.'

He raised the gun and pointed it in my direction.

I was beginning really to hate having guns pointed at me. 'Careful,' I said. 'Is that thing loaded?'

He nodded an affirmation.

I slowed, but didn't come to a halt completely. As I edged towards him, I saw that the gun was a huge old Webley & Scott – a big weapon, with a hell of a kick to it.

'Why did you have to stick your nose in?' asked Harvey.

If I'd been looking for any thanks for what I'd done, I was obviously going to be disappointed.

But what did I expect? In a sorry situation like this one, there was no credit for anyone. No winners, only losers.

'I didn't,' I said. 'I was invited to the party. I didn't want anything to do with it, believe me. Getting involved in all this again was the last thing I wanted.'

'Sharman,' said Byrne. 'I know that name.'

'I was a DC under you, years ago,' I said. 'When all this happened,' and I threw the paper at him.

It hit him in the chest, and he grabbed it, and looked at the front page in the light from the open front door. His face was in shadow, but I would have bet he paled when he saw it.

I heard him sigh, and he let the paper go, and it fluttered to the ground.

'I thought that was all forgotten,' he said.

Harvey turned the gun back on him at his words, much to my relief. 'Is it true?' he said bleakly.

Byrne didn't reply.

'Well is it?' His voice was louder then.

Byrne nodded.

'Then I'm going to kill you.'

'Don't waste a bullet on him,' I said. 'There are other ways.'

Harvey looked at me. 'Why did you have to come here?' he asked, and his voice was desperate.

On the other hand, I think Byrne was quite pleased I'd arrived. Maybe he thought that a third party, a witness, would help defuse the situation.

'Listen, Doug,' he said. 'Why don't you just put the gun down now? We can talk, have a drink.'

Harvey turned back in his direction. 'Shut up, you,' he said. 'Just shut up.'

'I'm sorry about what happened, Doug,' Byrne went on, ignoring what Harvey said. 'I really am. I don't know what came over me. I was suffering such stress at work at the time –'

'*Stress*. You bastard,' interrupted Harvey furiously. 'Stress.' His face seemed to crumple in on itself, and the gun shook in his hand, as if the weight of it was too much for him. Or the weight of something at least. 'I'll give you stress. I trusted you with my daughters, and you did what you did to them. What sort of stress have Jackie and I been under all these years? Answer me that.'

'I know,' said Byrne. 'What can I say?'

Not what you *are* saying, I thought. You're asking for trouble.

'Why don't you, Mr Harvey?' I said. 'Just put the gun down, please. It's all over for him and the rest of his crew.'

'What do you mean?' asked Byrne.

'I mean they're all dead. Collier and Millar were shot last night, and Grisham just threw himself under the nine-fifteen from Victoria.'

I didn't know what train it was, but the more I talked the better chance I had of Harvey putting the gun away without hurting anyone. Particularly me.

'Christ,' said Byrne.

'And you're finished too,' I said to him. 'You're going to go to prison for a long time, Mr ex-Assistant Commissioner. A very long time. And Sailor Grant told me what they do to people like you inside.' I looked at my watch. 'Put the gun down, Mr Harvey. The papers are out on the streets now, and his little game is up. Jacqueline wouldn't want you to go to prison. She needs all the support you can give her. This is not going to be an easy time.'

'Why did Jackie speak to you?' asked Harvey. 'Why after all this time did she choose some stranger to talk to? Why not me?'

I didn't tell him what she'd told me. About the way she thought he would have taken it. And the fact that she didn't trust him. That would have definitely driven him over the edge if anything would. 'It's easier with strangers. I just said the right things to her at the right time,' I said.

Pushed all the right buttons, in the right order, I thought. But I didn't tell him that either.

'Dead,' said Harvey. 'They're dead, you say.' And he smiled. A terrible death's head of a smile that contained not one degree of humour. 'That's good. I like that.'

'So there's no need for all this. Give me the gun, Doug,' I said, using his Christian name for the first time. 'No one needs to know you had it. He isn't going to tell.' I looked at Byrne. 'And I'm certainly not. We can call the police from here, and let them deal with it.'

I think he almost did too. Almost gave me the gun, and let the mills of justice, like the mills of God, begin to grind in their slow and small way.

Except Byrne didn't know when to keep his mouth shut.

'That's it, Doug,' he said. 'Listen to Sharman. He's right. Put the gun down. I'm sure we can sort everything out.'

His words hung in front of us like dry bones rattling together in a breeze that stank of corruption.

'No,' said Harvey. 'No more sorting things out. Not for you. Not for me. I've had enough of all that. No police. Not any more.'

And he pointed the pistol he was holding in his hand towards Byrne, and he pulled the trigger.

Once, twice, three times.

The gun belched gouts of orange flame, and the noise of the explosions crashed off the brickwork of the house, and echoed across the darkness of the long front garden, until they were lost in the trees that surrounded the property, and only the ringing in my ears reminded me of them.

The heavy calibre bullets ripped into Byrne's upper torso, blowing him back against the doorframe, where he stood erect for a moment, before falling forward to lie still on the smooth porch tiles.

Harvey stood for one brief second and looked at the fallen body of his brother-in-law, before, with a sort of half-smile in my direction, he put the hot barrel of the still-smoking gun into his mouth, and pulled the trigger one last time.

The bullet blew his head almost off his shoulders, and he dropped like a stone to lie next to Byrne.

In the silence that followed the noise, I stood alone.

So it was finally finished, I thought.

The dreadful events that had started all that time ago had finally come to their bloody conclusion.

Except for one detail.

I looked down at the two bodies lying next to the sheets of newsprint that Byrne had dropped, and took Toby Gillis's Browning out of my pocket and unwrapped it. I bent and put it carefully into Doug Harvey's inside coat pocket, trying not to catch the stink coming from his corpse or leave any of my prints on the gun.

It might not work, but at least it would confuse the issue.

As I stood up again, I heard the sound of a distant siren.

I'd have to tell Jackie what I'd done. And why. I was sure she'd understand in time.

At least, I hoped she would.

Pretend We're Dead

by Mark Timlin

The Tenth Nick Sharman novel

Sharman's getting married, and down at the nick they're taking bets on how long it's going to last.

But Dawn (the ex-stripper) isn't going to settle for little woman status – she's got her eye on those mean streets.

And Sharman's going to need all the help he can get with the little matter of a rock star twenty years dead who's back and wanting his royalties…

'It is possible that South London contains some law-abiding citizens in conventional relationships, but they make no appearance in Timlin's immoral, widely enjoyable books' – *Times*

'An intriguing plot, fast action, gritty detail and a consumption of alcohol that is excessive even by Mickey Spillane standards'
– *Evening Standard*

'dishes out his usual sleazy fast-read fun with tons of profane wit'
– *Time Out*

978-1-84344-628-6   £12.99

Paint It Black

by Mark Timlin

The Eleventh Nick Sharman novel

Nick Sharman – at last – is living a life of married bliss with his new partner (and ex-stripper) Dawn. The bad boy has settled down, and the booze and the drugs and the guns are but a happy memory – unlike his ex-wife Laura, now married to respectability.

Laura's quite capable of shattering the idyll, but this time it's serious – their fifteen-year-old daughter Judith, has gone missing. The police are looking, but have no leads and Laura fears the worst.

Sharman still has his own skills. But Laura's call catapults him back into a world he should have left behind. And when he decides to right some wrongs in his own way, domestic bliss becomes a thing of the past – and Sharman, once again, finds himself playing for keeps.

'The most impressive aspect of Timlin's compressed style is the constant juxtaposition of the witty and the tense' – *Loaded*

978-1-84344-685-9   £12.99

Find My Way Home

by Mark Timlin

The Twelfth Nick Sharman novel

Harry Stonehouse had been a cop, a good one – and straight, unlike Nick Sharman. After taking early retirement he'd landed a job at a security firm. Now he's dead, and his wife wants Nick to find out who killed him and why.

Nick's been taking a close look at hell recently and doesn't care too much about anything beyond the next Jack Daniel's. But Harry had been a friend, and Nick had screwed his wife and he feels sorry for her. Big mistake.

In an unlikely partnership with ex-DI Robber, escaping from resentful retirement at his sister's, Sharman sets off in pursuit – and finds himself swept along in the deadly aftermath of a £20 million heist. And with that much money at stake, betrayal, double-crossing and murder are just for starters…

'Mean streets, sleazy bars, beutal bent coppers … as British as a used condom in a fogbound London taxi' – *Observer*

978-1-84344-689-7   £12.99

About Us

In addition to No Exit Press, Oldcastle Books has a number of other imprints, including Kamera Books, Creative Essentials, Pulp! The Classics, Pocket Essentials and High Stakes Publishing > oldcastlebooks.co.uk

For more information about Crime Books go to > crimetime.co.uk

Check out the kamera film salon for independent, arthouse and world cinema > kamera.co.uk

For more information, media enquiries and review copies please contact Frances > frances@oldcastlebooks.com